Enjoy

of Manomet's

own

WICKED MOON

Taylor

Nash

10/14

Published by Ida Kay Miller, Savoy, IL

Printed in the United States of America on acid-free paper.

2014

First Edition

Ida Kay Miller
P. O. Box 760
Savoy, IL 61874-0760

DEDICATION

My incredible son, daughter-in-law, and granddaughters—
Cory, Heather, Marissa, and Olivia

I love you so much and you bring me immeasurable joy!

***

Mother, my siblings, their spouses, nieces and nephews—
My sister, Karen—the strongest woman I know and an
inspiration to all!

I'm blessed to have you all in my life. Love you!

***

My wonderful friends—

*You know who you are! Thanks for the journey and taking me
along for the ride!!*

***

*And those that have passed before us—we miss you every
day, but know we'll all be together again.*

ACKNOWLEDGEMENT

I could write a separate book to acknowledge and thank those who played some part in the production of *Wicked Moon*. I appreciate your support and couldn't have done it without you! Love and hugs to all!

Randy Parker
Ida Kay Parker
Kristin Orr
Terri Valentine
Jennifer Clements
Karen Macken
Karen & **Ken** Buechs
Cathy Gorman

Mary Ellen Parker
Amy Davies
Cindy Schilling
Cris Heinrich
Tillie DuBois
Alstena Calvetti
Stanley Mazalewski
Elysia Shanahan

Thanks to the local businesses for allowing me to use your names so *Wicked Moon* is more realistic to the Manomet area:

The Simes Foundation
The Lobster Pound
Brewers Boat Yard
Manomet Library
Stowell's Café and Deli
Gellar's Snackbar

The Blue Spruce Motel
Priscilla Beach Theatre
Katsura Gardens
Marshlands
Tidmarsh Farms

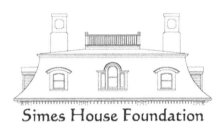

Simes House Foundation

Wicked Moon is purely a work of fiction and labor of love. The setting is a real house called the Simes House. The location is the wonderful coastal village of Manomet in the Town of Plymouth, Massachusetts which is ringed by the Pine Hills, peppered with ponds, and fronted by Cape Cod Bay. The roads, landmarks, and businesses in *Wicked Moon* all exist.

The Simes House is a rare, unusually ornate Mansard roof Italianate Victorian built in 1863. She was built by Joseph Simes, a wealthy transportation and investment magnate, as his summer resort. In old New England, buildings of such vintage are not generally considered especially aged or significant. Known to natives as the Manomet Mansion, over the years she fell into disrepair. Her massive size was no match for pockets wanting, but her granite was flush, her bones strong, floors level, and walls plumb. She was worth saving.

The House and her remaining acre of land were taken for taxes. In 2010 the town proposed an article to tear her down and build subsidized housing. Villagers argued to Town Meeting that the Manomet Village Master Plan looked to preserve the village's unique, historical features, and to create a village green in the vicinity of Point and State Roads. It was like a gift dropped from heaven, noticed, and meant to fulfill a prophecy of village unity and identity. Town Meeting declined the new housing, the non-profit Simes House Foundation was established, and a $1.5 million Community Preservation grant voted by Town Meeting toward historical restoration. The first floor is reserved for community events, upper stories for offices and apartments to sustain the premises. The yard is now Manomet Commons, there for all to enjoy.

Wicked Moon is inspired by the aura of the old home and the grass roots effort to save her. More resources are needed to complete the House and Commons. Profits from this book are dedicated to the effort, and you can be part of it too.

The Simes House and Manomet Commons can be visited at 29 Manomet Point Road, Plymouth, MA.

Arrangements for tours or events can be made at directors@simeshousefoundation.org.

A virtual tour, membership in the Foundation, history, pictures and apparel can be found by visiting the website www.simeshousefoundation.org/.

Other Books by
Taylor Nash

The Apparition

* * *

Uncharted Depths

*Winner Reader Views Literary
Award
Honorary Mention
Romance Category*

WICKED MOON

TAYLOR NASH

PROLOGUE

Manomet, Massachusetts
1884

No, Father," Belinda Eldridge exclaimed. "I will not give up my child."

"Yes, you will, young lady," Captain Sam Eldridge replied. "There will be no bastard child raised in this digging, regardless of what your mother said. You will not keep this child. You are nothing more than a strumpet."

She stomped out of the bedroom fit for a princess on the second floor of the family's mansion, down the mahogany-trimmed, curved staircase. She ran down the steps faster than prudent, but she ignored safety in favor of escaping her unreasonable father.

"Where do you think you're going, Belinda Sue?" he yelled. He descended the spiral staircase. "You come back. We're not finished with this conversation. There's no way in hell you're leaving this house—now or ever."

She tripped a few steps away from the bottom stair. Her hand trembled when she grabbed for the banister at the same moment her father's fingers closed tightly around her arm.

He wasn't trying to keep her from falling. He was doing everything in his power to keep her from leaving. If she got outside, she'd never come back to her mean, controlling father.

She yanked away her arm which enabled her to reach the glass knob. Her father slipped on the stair. The heavy door swung open and slammed into the wall, allowing the strong November wind to fill the vestibule.

The frigid air forced its way beneath her flannel robe and nightgown, chilling her to the bone. Or, perhaps it was the fear of her father and what he might do to her and her unborn child. He would never let her marry a man of her choosing, especially Joshua.

"Belinda, stop," he yelled. He tried to regain his footing.

She dashed barefoot across the frozen lawn; her toes tingled from the bitter cold. Her father's labored breathing indicated he was close behind. The thorny, wild rosebushes caught her robe. If she could reach the bluff and get down the stairs, he'd never find her in Joshua's cave, their love nest recessed amongst the dense trees.

Asthma caused her chest to tighten and made it difficult to catch her breath. She stumbled over a large branch that had fallen in the recent storm. Hands and knees soiled and bloodied from the spill, she fled with renewed intensity until she reached the bluff blanketed with ivy.

Even though her father had been drinking heavily earlier, he caught up and blocked her entrance to the stairs that led to the strip of beach far below. Her pregnant condition had slowed her down.

"Father, you can't take my child away from me. I love my baby and would do anything to keep it safe. I love Joshua. He's coming back for us. We're going to get married, be a family. You'll see."

"No, he's not, Belinda." He placed his hands on his knees to support his body, puffs of mist released into the frigid air. "He's nothing more than a no-account mud sill. His boat sank in that nor'easter fifty miles out. He's dead and you can't raise this child alone. I forbid it. You and the baby will be a disgrace to this family. You will go to a home and put this bastard up for adoption. This is the devil's work."

"No, I won't. He is coming back. You're lying to me. They never found his body. You'd do anything to keep me away from Joshua, I know you would. Mother said she'd help me."

When he approached, she stepped back toward the cliff. Her left foot slid underneath a tangled, thorny locust tree. She lost her balance, causing her to fall backwards.

"No, Belinda, no," her father shrieked as he extended his arm.

She reached out, his fingers inches away. Her body reeled seaward with a sense of timelessness and suspended animation.

"No, please God, no." The hysterical tone in his voice echoed over the water.

The winds whirled around her as though attempting to soften her fall. The radiant full moon illuminated the sky; speckles of stars dotted darkness. Waves crashed on the jetty below and echoed in her ears.

Her nightgown fluttered in the wind while her body made the descent. Her back faced the rocks eighty feet below. She swathed her arms around her distended abdomen, holding her precious baby she loved more than life itself. She wailed silently within, but was peaceful as she embraced her impending doom, accepting a fate beyond the reality threatened by her parochial sire.

Instead of seeing the man in the moon, Joshua's face appeared. His eyes beckoned before she hit House Rock.

CHAPTER 1

Kelli Goddard's stomach tensed when she recalled the letter she received two weeks ago. Compelled to deal with the property tax issue herself on her inherited mansion on Cape Cod Bay, she turned into the uneven rocky driveway on Manomet Point Road just as dusk set in. Intertwined, overgrown knotweed had created an impenetrable barrier that hid the old mansion from the two-lane road. She slowly crept up the winding drive.

At the top of the driveway, she came to a halt. The silhouette of the house reminded her of a horror flick movie set. The dilapidated mansion had obviously been neglected too long. No lights were on, inside or out. An upstairs window had been boarded on the top quarter panel, crooked steps and a slanted porch obvious even in the growing darkness.

Something creaked, maybe a shutter, maybe not. Goosebumps traveled up her arm and caressed her spine. Not knowing what she faced, her breathing quickened.

She parked and rolled up the window in her decade old Jeep and grabbed the bulky flashlight from the cracked leather passenger seat. She had been afraid of the dark since a small child. Her pulse quickened. Fallen tree limbs, uneven stones, and warped steps caused her balance to falter. It was as if the old house warned her to leave. Nevertheless, she bravely faced the ten-foot double wooden doors.

Imposing overgrown lilacs and wisteria, tangled with bittersweet, swayed with the strong north wind and clamored like a woman with long nails, scraping wood on the side of the house. The wind swirled restlessly and sounds emitted from the interior.

Was someone whining or crying? No, it was just her imagination.

With fumbling cold fingers, despite it being late June, she propped the flashlight between her bare knees and struggled with the padlock. After several attempts to unlock it, she tried to force it only for the padlock to smash her stiff ring finger before giving in.

"Damn," she muttered, shaking her injured appendage. Then she mustered all her strength to push open the cumbrous doors. Rusted hinges creaked loudly. Her ears vibrated.

She hated to admit, but she was scared shitless. Her heart beat fast and hard; she held her breath. She focused the flashlight beam up the massive curved staircase, catching a red reflection at the top. Was that Belinda, the ghost she'd seen as a child? Strong drafts hurled dust and debris through the ray.

The batteries in the flashlight weakened and drained fast. If there had been moonlight, it might have helped her strained eyes. She'd driven over twenty hours straight from Illinois.

A board creaked on the second floor. A piercing wail reverberated throughout the house. She quivered. Maybe she should leave and come back tomorrow during daylight?

Without warning, a crushing blow smashed the side of her head. Luminous streaks of light flashed around her as the darkness overtook her.

~ ~ ~

When Kelli woke, her head pulsated which quickly reminded her something serious had happened. Her eyes darted around the pristine white room. She searched for anything familiar. An IV machine beeped next to her. Doctors and nurses scurried in the hall with stethoscopes draped around their necks.

Why am I here?

"Miss Goddard?" The doctor strolled into the room with a small laptop in his hand. "I'm Doctor Brown and you're one lucky lady." He stepped closer and made eye contact. "If that blow had been a quarter of an inch closer to your temple, I'm afraid the outcome would have been significantly different. The CT scan didn't show any swelling of the brain, which is remarkable given the size of the wound to your skull."

"What happened?" Her fingertips recognized the gauze surface which covered the side of her head, the wound tender to the touch. "I don't remember anything."

The young intern stepped to the right side of her bed, leaned down and flashed a bright light in each eye temporarily blinding her. "That's not uncommon with head injuries, ma'am. Actually, Officer Scott is here to ask a few questions, or I can tell him to come back tomorrow."

Acid swelled in her throat. Her body was sore, reminding her of the time she'd flipped over the handlebars of her bicycle at twelve.

"You have a concussion, so you may experience dizziness, nausea, or blurred vision, all normal symptoms. We're going to keep you overnight for observation," the doctor said. "I'll let the officer in, but just for a few minutes. If you need anything, let the nurse know. I'll check on you tomorrow morning."

Before she could reply, a man, oddly familiar, in a blue uniform entered.

"Officer Scott," Dr. Brown said, "you may find she perseverates or repeats herself. You have five minutes and that's all."

She rearranged her body in the uncomfortable hospital bed. Each move caused a throbbing pain.

"Kelli, it's Gregg. Officer Gregg Scott now. Didn't think we'd be meeting up after all these years like this."

"Gregg?"

"Sorry about the accident. Heard rumors you were coming back to handle the probate for Hattie and do something with the mansion."

Gregg Scott. Of course. She hadn't seen him in at least thirty years, but she would never forget those baby blue eyes. And, how she'd felt about him at one time.

"What happened? I don't remember anything?"

"A passerby found you lying on Point Road unconscious and bleeding from the head. Thought you'd been involved in a hit and run, but doctors said that was unlikely with your head wound and no abrasions or broken bones. Were you walking on the road? We're hoping you could shed some light on what occurred."

"Side of the road?" She lightly ran her fingers through her tangled hair; flecks of blood dislodged and fell on her loosely-fitting hospital gown that would expose all if she stood up.

"Try to remember, Kelli."

She closed her eyes and laid her head against the pillow. "All I recall is going to the mansion. Just got into town and was anxious. I went inside and that's the last I remember."

"Were you alone?"

"Yes."

"Did you see anyone or hear anything?"

When she opened her eyes, two of everything danced around the room which caused her to be woozy and queasy. "No. It was dark and windy. Did someone hit me on the head?"

"Doctor said you got a dandy blow. Who would've known you were there? Maybe some plaster from the ceiling fell on you? But that doesn't explain how you got back down the road."

A petite nurse entered the room. "Officer, I'm afraid you must leave. Doctor wants Ms. Goddard to rest now." The woman grabbed her wrist and checked for a pulse.

"Kelli, we'll get to the bottom of this. Where are you staying?"

"The Blue Spruce, but haven't checked in yet."

"Once you're feeling up to it, we'll need to interview you. If you need a ride when you're discharged, let me know." He handed her his card. "Nice to have you back in town. Sorry you got off to a rough start."

"Thanks, Gregg. My car?"

"It's parked in front of the mansion. It's not going anywhere." He exited the room with a familiar lazy gait she recalled from their teenage days. Apparently, over the years he'd gained extra weight, especially the bulging midsection that obscured his belt. A fan of locally brewed beer, no doubt, or maybe too many donuts. Then she frowned.

Why would someone want to hurt me?

CHAPTER 2

It was against Kelli's better judgment to return to the mansion that sat on eighty acres since her release from the hospital that morning, but she went anyway. Her head throbbed, which caused occasional bouts of an upset stomach and light-headedness. Regardless, no one was going to frighten her away that easily.

She retraced events of last night, straining to recollect details. She remembered unlocking the cumbersome padlock, stepping into the front door, but everything from that point forward was void. The doctor acknowledged amnesia was common with head injuries.

In daylight the condition of the mansion was far worse than anticipated. It probably wasn't the smartest idea to go back so soon, but she was driven to resolve the back tax issue.

Aunt Hattie had been forced into a nursing home due to Alzheimer's and Multiple Sclerosis before she died. She had put her home in a management trust years ago and had been well cared for. She had been shocked at the memorial service to learn the town had taken the mansion for back taxes. Notices were ignored by the company in charge. Nobody was around to be held accountable for not paying the bills since they had closed their doors.

The good news was the final judgment was never issued. She managed to beg and borrow enough bucks for back taxes, even though her financial situation was dire, so she could save the house. She had to. Hattie had left the mansion to her. She loved Hattie and the house. As long as she had the house, she'd always have Hattie.

Coping with her husband's death and financial issues had been all she could handle, but she was guilt-ridden. She should have stayed closer to her aunt, been there. One thing led to another, like these BKC Properties people, filing for title before final judgment. They thought they owned the house. BKC jumped the gun. Now it was her turn.

A black Denali sat in the side yard which concerned her, but she was determined to go into the house anyway.

Gray streaked stairs were slivered and fractured. Afraid to tumble, she grasped the unsteady flaking banister. How stupid had she been to navigate in the dark? She could've been injured or worse just trying to get into the house last night.

Discolored maroon double doors were open, exposing the spectacular palatial curved staircase, its allurement undeniable. It'd always been her favorite spot in the house. Happy memories surged back to the days when she was a child and played on the manicured grounds of the Manomet Mansion where Aunt Hattie had lived. She'd pretend to be a bride and wore old slips or torn dresses that trailed when she descended the lengthy stairs.

The square brown, blue, and tan tile vestibule had been a favorite hiding place from her brother, Blake. Holding her breath in anticipation of being found, she'd study the rare etched glass panes on the doors and count the tiles until he discovered her.

And now Blake was gone forever too.

Did I leave the doors open or did the officers? How could I have stumbled to the street if I was unconscious? Even though confused and alarmed by what happened her first night in Manomet, she loved the quaint village she considered a second home.

Two men lingered in the wide center hallway next to the majestic staircase with clipboards and pens, intent on their discussion. That explained the Denali parked in the side yard.

The man in the tailored suit caught her attention immediately. He was strikingly handsome and well built. Her heart fluttered. It wasn't right to be attracted to another man since her husband died. Was it?

"Excuse me. Who are you and why are you in my house?" Her head pounded in unison to each word.

"Excuse me, ma'am, but this isn't your house," he answered.

She couldn't believe the deep tone in his voice rattled her nerves, melting her insides. She guessed him to be close to her age, late forties, well dressed. The other man, who appeared to be in his mid-twenties, chuckled, which automatically set her emotionally on fire. Not that it would take much today.

"Yes, it is," she stubbornly replied. "It's a tangled hell of a mess, but I've been assured by my legal representatives when it's all done and said, this is my house."

A fresh stream of sweat broke out on the man's brow.

"I inherited it from my aunt."

"This property belongs to BKC Properties," the mature man replied.

"And do *you* represent BKC Properties?" She didn't care how flustered she was, she'd stand her ground.

"Yes, I'm part owner of BKC and project manager. And may I ask who you are?"

"Kelli Goddard. This is my home. I didn't authorize you or anyone else access to it."

"I'm sorry about the legal confusion, but our company now owns the property. We paid the back taxes," he replied, retreating to the dusty staircase.

Why were the fine hairs on the back of her neck raised? It wasn't her nature to be snippy when meeting someone for the first time. Was it the tone in their voices, wealthy attire, or could they be connected to the unknown attacker who struck her? Or was it her distrust of men in general because of what her husband had done?

"We'll see who's confused." She retrieved her cell, pulled out a business card and dialed. While the phone rang, she strolled into the front parlor. Distraught over the poor condition of the room that held tender memories, her stomach tightened.

"Gregg, Kelli here. I'm at the house. I've got a problem. There's some man here who claims he owns it. I have no clue who the asshole is, but can you come over and get him out...*now?*"

Was she putting up a front of wanting him out of her house when she actually wanted to jump into his arms?

What's wrong with me? Why is he having this effect on me? This is insane.

"Be there in five. Stay calm, Kelli," Officer Scott responded.

She scanned the parlor. The morning sun reflected off the old mirror above the antique handcrafted fireplace. There were twelve throughout the house, some more ornate than others, but this was her favorite.

When she visited in the winter, she'd sit in this room with Auntie. A roaring, crackling fire spewed scents of cedar mixed with cherry throughout the house while wind and snow whipped snowdrifts outside. They'd sip homemade hot chocolate topped with tiny colored marshmallows, both wrapped in knitted afghans made by Auntie.

She was livid with the condition the trust had left the house. When Auntie was forced into the nursing home, her keep was assured by automatic withdrawals against the property. Hattie had been adamant she should never sell the property, but the place was tapped.

But then, so was she.

Or maybe the town had tried to reach her? Had she been so overwhelmed with her husband's death, maybe phone messages were erased? Was it her fault?

The fixed transom double French doors leading to the one-story covered veranda were ajar. The solid glass was intact above and on the doors, but foggy and smudged from accumulated sea salt and wind; bottom wood panels had not weathered well, splintered, peeling, and warped.

"Kelli?" Officer Scott entered the parlor without knocking. "So explain again what the problem is."

"They're walking around the dining room now. The door must not have been locked. Think they had something to do with the attack?" She paced.

"Slow down, Kelli."

"They don't believe I inherited the mansion. There's been a major screw up somewhere. They said BKC Properties owns it now. The arrogant jerk is in there. Would you please get them out of my house? Like now. I don't need any more frustration in my life right now."

"Okay, remember—you're still recovering," Officer Scott instructed. "Let me check out what's going on."

The men entered the parlor, laughing and shaking their heads. "Hi, Officer. Hope you can set the record straight. She's under the impression she owns this house. You may or may not know, BKC Properties acquired it a few days ago for the back taxes."

"Now you folks are going to have to hold on here. Kelli inherited the Manomet Mansion from her Aunt Hattie. I assume you two represent the condominium builder who's bought land up and down the Cape?"

"Sorry, Officer, and...young lady. How rude of me. Rod Kesson and this is my assistant, Brock Grey. I'm an owner of BKC Properties and, yes, we develop luxury condominiums. I've placed a call to my legal team. They'll investigate. I'm sure they'll get it squared away, but I can assure you we're the rightful owners of this property."

"Hattie Hubbard was my aunt. She passed away and left the mansion to me." Her voice wavered, not just from anger, but from his presence. She had to remind herself he was the enemy here.

"Obviously, there's some confusion. The town noticed and took for non-payment of taxes, so my corporation redeemed it. I'm sorry about your aunt, but this was a legal transaction and the property rightly belongs to my company. As a matter of fact, we're going to demolish this wreck within a week or so."

"Demolish it? Condominiums? No friggin' way."

"Sorry, lady, but you can't stop progress. You can't stop me."

"Progress? The hell with progress. I've had about all the progress I need in this lifetime. Someone knocks me out cold last night. Bet BKC Properties doesn't know anything about that either, do they? I'll fight you to the end over this. This property has been and will be passed down for generations. That was my aunt's final wish. You'll be hearing from my attorneys." She clenched her fists until her knuckles were white.

"I don't know what you're referring to about last night, but on the legal end of the matter, we'll let the attorneys battle this one out...but you'll lose. The papers have been signed and recorded. The town can't renege. They got their money. Plus, I've got almost all the units sold, which means a large increase in revenue for Plymouth."

Her blood pressure elevated which caused her injured head to ache. Infuriated with this stranger—it was not what he said, but the tone—arrogant, smirky, and so assured he was right. So, why was she attracted to him?

"The only way you're touching my house is over my dead body."

So, why did he just smile?

CHAPTER 3

Rod Kesson sat in his multi-million customized Prevost motor coach which overlooked Cape Cod Bay. The expansive wrap-around windshield allowed a picturesque view of the cloudless sky. A slight breeze filtered through the open side windows. It was so clear he recognized Provincetown and the monument at the end of the point.

A lifelong resident in Manomet had converted an empty lot next to his cottage for a motor coach. Not able to travel anymore since his eyesight failed from macular degeneration, the owner rented the pad for a hefty price, usually to summer tourists.

Rod had thought it odd someone would go to the trouble and expense of installing a sewer, water line, and fifty amp electrical until he heard the monthly charge. He respected the man's business savvy, capitalizing on this prime location, even if it was at his company's expense. When undertaking development projects of this magnitude, he preferred his motor coach within five miles, so he could be hands-on day or night.

His custom made one-hundred-foot Hatteras yacht was docked at Brewers Boat Yard in Plymouth, fifteen minutes from his coach, which allowed him to slip away at a moment's notice. The ostentatious craft served as a hub for procuring investors for condominium projects. Prospective clients enjoyed the lavish treatment, even though some never intended to part with their bayside property. They were accustomed to lobster boats or small recreational sailboats, nothing of this caliber, but attended the 'by invitation only' meetings out of curiosity and to indulge in expensive hors d'oeuvres and cocktails.

"Troy, Rod here. We've got a problem with the Manomet Mansion. Some lady showed up and claimed she inherited the house from her aunt. I need an answer ASAP, like yesterday, what the hell's going on. You know we've got investors lined up ready to sign off on this project plus the demolition crew," he explained. He propped his brown Calvin Klein loafers on the handcrafted cherry desk.

"Not possible," Attorney Troy Adkins replied. "We dotted our i's and crossed our t's on this deal, even though Barker had to pull strings to get 'er done so quickly. For what we paid under the table to get this accomplished, there better not be any damn problems. Let me get on it and I'll get back to you."

"Sounds like a plan. I'll wait anxiously and, meanwhile, I'll keep the crew ready to go with the demolition. Assume it won't take long to get the permits?"

"Nope. Double checked and zoning apps are already completed and ready to be submitted. Operations said they had to supply square footage and a plan that showed what's coming down and interim treatment. They'll determine fill, grading, temp loam and seed once we give them the development plans. Guess biggest issue is utilities have to be disconnected and the power company takes forever."

"Great. Let's get this baby down and ramp up construction. Interest is compounding, so we don't have time to sit on this project. Time is money—mine."

"I'll be in touch."

"And, please don't mention this to Dad. I don't need him breathing down my neck until we know what happened. You know how he panics and sure don't want to give him another heart attack."

"Gotcha."

"Probably should mention I got questioned by local police. The lady, who claims she owns the mansion, was attacked on the property and hit in the head. Surprised they questioned me, but thought since we had a conflict over the property, I was a person of interest. Dumb shits. How stupid do they think we are?"

"Grasping for straws, that's all. You know, you don't have to answer any questions unless I'm there."

"Yeah, but there's no reason not to cooperate. Okay, Troy. Get back to me."

"You bet. Later, Rod."

Deep in contemplation, he massaged his stubbly chin, playing with a small skin tag on the bottom which annoyed him.

The lady was feisty, not to mention attractive in a girl-next-door sorta way. He bet they were close in age; he'd turn fifty-two in a few months.

His typical woman was much younger, socially adept, and model material, capturing attention of any man when she entered a room. Miss…he couldn't remember her name…was a plain Jane, but she did have a special attraction he couldn't put his finger on. Her height was close to five-foot-six, giving her the nerve to stand up to his six-foot-two frame. A little too padded for him. Probably weighed one-hundred-thirty pounds.

Beautiful women didn't challenge him. Most bent over backwards to date the mighty Rod Kesson, the eligible and wealthiest bachelor on the East Coast, not to mention heir to billions from his father's companies and mother's inherited wealth from generations. Once he came close to tying the knot to get his parents off his back. An only child, he was responsible for a slew of grandchildren. His short-term fiancée wasn't tolerant of his relaxed standards back then and called off the wedding at the last minute. It totally embarrassed and broke his parents' hearts, another notch on his father's belt of how he had disappointed him.

Now that he was older, he regretted not having children to pass on the family legacy. He'd never have the opportunity to raise a child with unconditional love, having never learned that from his father.

His main aspiration in life was to surpass his father's fortune and prove to be a more astute businessman. To put an end to the competition with his father who constantly compared him to other professional men, usually in demeaning ways, to get his goat or push him to the next level of success. Was he becoming like his father, Phil? Was the cycle repeating through each generation? It was well known his grandfather had been a ruthless son-of-a-bitch.

His mother, Dartha, on the other hand, was the most compassionate woman he'd ever known. He respected and loved her dearly. Born and raised in North Carolina, she had an eloquent southern drawl that captivated him. She was a feisty, petite woman who hardly reached five foot, a real steel magnolia. If anybody could make his father spin on his heels, it was his mother, a simple glare sufficient.

As a child she'd read to him every night, her soothing voice instantly lulling him to sleep. Even after all these years, he could listen to her for hours; her endearing love spilled out with every word.

His parents were the ideal couple. Father ran the businesses and finances. Mother oversaw the house and estate, with help, of course. She volunteered for charities, especially those connected to needy children. Her socializing complemented his father's business ventures.

Maybe he didn't have a life partner, but he couldn't imagine his sophisticated legal team would've missed a detail where some woman *might* own the mansion. That complication had never crossed his mind.

Okay, sail, fish, golf or check out the attractive, aggressive lady at the mansion? He smiled a wolfish grin.

The lady always wins.

CHAPTER 4

Emotionally drained from her injury and confrontation yesterday, Kelli crawled out of bed later than planned. She'd not slept well. She woke up thinking about the dark haired, arrogant man. She smiled at the thought but wanted to scream at the same time. She did not have time for this kind of foolishness. She needed to be strong and take care of herself for a change.

She tugged aside the heavy curtain. The radiant Massachusetts sunshine temporarily blinded her. The window was slightly ajar; fresh air infiltrated the room.

Accommodations at the Blue Spruce Motel, which was a couple of blocks from the mansion, were not only convenient and outstanding, but had character and charm. Every morning it served a continental breakfast including homemade muffins.

The owner's residence was in the white building on the north side. The south end had been converted to an office and breakfast station. The homey atmosphere welcomed guests from all over the United States and Canada.

"Good mornin', Kelli," Tom greeted cheerfully. An antique roll-top desk behind the counter displayed pictures of his family.

She was amazed the owners remembered each patron's name. The motel appeared to be close to capacity with cars lined up in front of the single-story beige buildings and townhouses. Summer was prime time for tourists on the Cape.

"Good morning. See Cheryl's been at it again. You know, by the time I get done staying here I'm going to gain twenty pounds with all her home cooking."

"Well, we're glad you enjoy it," he acknowledged in a Bostonian accent. "How'd it go at the house yesterday and how's your head? Police have any idea who attacked you?"

"I won't go into detail, but looks like I've got bigger problems than who hit me, if you can believe that. Possession problem, to be exact."

She loaded her plastic tray with fresh coffee, cream, sugar, homemade hot muffins, a banana, and orange juice. She wondered if the fireplace was original, but was sure the mirror above had been added later.

"Police are investigating. They threw out the crazy idea plaster dislodged and fell on me."

"Really. Knew the mansion was in disrepair, but doesn't sound logical. I'm sure you'll get it squared away." He stepped around the counter and refilled the coffee.

Outside, she delighted in the fresh cool air of the summer morning. The wrought iron table sets underneath the old drive-through allowed patrons to enjoy the sunlight, breakfast, and clean Manomet air.

The eating area was surrounded by geraniums, impatiens, knock-out roses, and permanent bushes which added to the ambiance. She noticed an open patio above when she walked over which was formed into a V. Was it a private patio for the owners?

It wasn't humid like her hometown of Broward, Illinois. With a slight breeze from the ocean, the sweet scent of indigenous spruce accentuated the air.

In spite of her surrounding, she still fumed. She picked up her phone to see if she had cell service, which fluctuated hourly.

One of these days the cell providers should figure out how to put boosters on channel buoys.

"Rossen Law Firm."

"Hi. This is Kelli Goddard. May I speak to Richard, please?"

"I'm sorry. Mr. Rossen is on vacation for two weeks. Is there something I can help you with?" the cheerful receptionist asked.

"Two weeks?" she cried out. "I've got a real problem here. Will he be calling in? It's urgent I talk to him and only him."

"He's out of the country. I can probably send an e-mail, but I'm guessing it'll be a couple of days before I get a response. What message would you like me to give him?"

"Crap…tell him to contact me immediately. You have my cell number on file. Tell him there's a possession or title problem with the Manomet Mansion. A company called BKC Properties is claiming ownership."

"I'm sure he'll be able to get this resolved, Mrs. Goddard. I'll send him an e-mail when we're done and one of us will be in touch when I hear from him. Is there anything else I can do to assist you?"

"No, that should take care of it. Thanks and please, please tell him how urgent this is. This is really stressing me out."

"You're welcome and I certainly will."

The phone went dead in her hand. Why did she feel stranded on a deserted island with no boat, no help, nowhere to turn? Her headache was back.

Haven't I been through enough and now this? My brother died. Then Steve's death five years ago and losing everything financially. Then Auntie passed and left me the mansion in total disrepair with no money to fix it, but expects me to keep it for future generations. And now the tax issue. What in the world am I going to do?

She exhaled several times which caused her chest to shudder. Somewhere in those dark clouds there had to be a silver lining. What was that saying? *God never gives you more than you can handle?* He must think she was one bad-ass chick.

Steaming coffee flowed down her throat and, hopefully, worked its magic giving a much needed energy boost. It was going to be next to impossible to restore the mansion. If—it belonged to her.

What a shame her mother and Auntie had been estranged all those years. Neither ever explained why. Someone in the family should have been overseeing the property. Maybe the situation would have turned out differently?

Once Auntie entered the nursing home, it appeared no one cared, except her and Captain Maz, her lifelong companion. But, with all that was going on in her life, she couldn't be there for Auntie when she needed her the most. It was tough. Over time Auntie physically and mentally declined from the wretched diseases. When she reached the point where her muscles became rigid and swallowing was impaired, there was no choice but to put her in a nursing home.

Her mother, stubborn as the day was long, made every excuse not to visit Hattie in her final years, even to the point of discouraging her without good explanation. When she got older, the issue caused friction between her and her mother. When her mother made up her mind on something, there was no changing it.

When Auntie passed away a year ago, the mansion was bequeathed to her, even though Hattie had a niece and nephew on her brother's side. She wasn't close to them since they didn't take time to stay connected.

Isolation from family and friends back home panicked her. She required security, stability, someone to trust and lean on. She was blessed with dear friends in Illinois and her son and his family in Indiana who would help in a heartbeat. Burdening them would never happen—if she could help it. Who could she turn to now that Steve had died?

She sighed. She had only herself to rely on now. Not very comforting since she had been attacked.

Maybe she'd startled someone in the mansion and that was why they attacked her? So many unanswered questions swirled through her brain.

Could the assault be connected to the gorgeous, aggravating man whose property company staked their claim? The local police, other than Gregg, didn't seem too concerned with following up quickly.

Stop, Kelli. Just stop. You can't torture yourself and put yourself under this much pressure. You can't save the world in one fell swoop. Stop dreaming about Mr. BKC. You're only asking for more trouble.

CHAPTER 5

Kelli wasn't waiting for an attorney or anyone to acknowledge the mansion was legally hers. This house was her heart and soul. When Auntie's health failed, she made her promise it'd be kept in the family for future generations. If her mother was alive and they'd reconciled, would the house have been bestowed to her mom?

Repeated notices from the town threatening possession for back taxes had been sent to the management company. Unbeknownst to her, the company folded, leaving renters in the home with no one in charge of maintenance, repairs, and paying the bills. Eventually, all services were shut off.

She unbolted the padlock on the front doors, admiring the authentic etched stained glass designed like crosses. Her finger followed the deep impressions. Perhaps those crosses sustained the house all those years, even though it hadn't protected her the other night.

It inevitably took her breath away when she entered the foyer. The baluster on the massive staircase was solid as the day it was hand carved. Decorative white spindles accented the deepness of the wood. The two-toned cherry and oak floor had been scratched over decades, but the color remained rich and deep. She never remembered a board creaking, until the other night.

Through the etched glass appeared a blurry figure, so she cracked the door.

"Yes? I'm sorry, I forgot your name." Her blood pressure soared.

He extended his hand. She ignored it. No way was she going to touch this man. She needed to get rid of him before her thoughts took her other places she shouldn't visit.

"Rod Kesson, ma'am."

"Kelli Goddard. Rightful owner of this home," she declared, her attitude indignant.

"Nice to see you again, Ms. Goddard, even if it's under these circumstances."

His remark reminded her of someone attending a funeral. "There are no circumstances, Mr. Kesson. I own this home. I intend to move forward with renovations."

"I've contacted my attorney and asked him to check into this situation immediately. Hopefully, we'll have some answers within a few days." He shuffled at the front door since she purposely hadn't invited him in.

"I've also contacted my legal counsel, and he assured me there is no way there can be dual ownership. I'm the rightful heir of this property," she lied.

"I'm sure we'll get it resolved. I don't mean to overstep my bounds, but do they know anything more about your accident in the house?"

"I didn't have an *accident*. Someone hit me over the head. You wouldn't know about that, would you?"

"Why would I? Perhaps something fell from the ceiling?" He looked up. "Appears there's water damage throughout the house. With the way the wind whipped the other night, maybe that's a possibility? I can't imagine why someone would attack you."

"Oh, you can't? How about a company that claims they own my property and perhaps wanted to scare me out of town? Gee, that's the first thing that came to my mind—and the police. Who else would have a motive, Mr. Kesson?" She nervously shifted in place.

"Please, call me Rod."

"Well, Rod, I don't think we need to be on a first name basis, but if you insist, it's Kelli."

He extended his hand again. This time she shook it hesitantly. It was warm and strong like his personality, which caused her to be guarded. Suddenly, she wanted those strong arms around her.

"Guess it'd be rude of me not to invite you in." What was she thinking? Why did she just let him back into the mansion?

"Since I'm here, it would be nice to see more of the house. I've only seen part of the downstairs."

"I'm not doing tours today or anytime until the house is refurbished. You're welcome to look around on your own if you're willing to sign a hold harmless, advised by my attorney. You know how attorneys are? Oh, and watch those loose boards on the second floor bath."

"So, your aunt owned this home? It's a shame she neglected it, allowing it to get in such terrible condition. The old lady looks like she was a real goddess once."

His voice grated on her nerves. Or was it just her perception, or emotional and mental state? Or her being aggravated at herself for finding him so damn attractive.

"This home has strong bones, even though right now it's disguised cosmetically decrepit."

Dressed immaculately with not a wrinkle in his blue silk shirt and black slacks, his aura and disposition reflected wealth, prominence, and education. His sensuous cologne wasn't one she recognized but contained musk. She liked musk.

There was no way he was from this area, probably not Boston, unless a transplant. His captivating southern drawl was a giveaway and indicated the lower East Coast, maybe Carolinas, Georgia, or Florida.

"My Aunt Hattie did the best with the resources she had. She became ill and was forced into a nursing home. A management company was in charge of the house but went belly up, leaving tenants and the house unattended. They absconded with anything of value, including some of her antique furniture and personal possessions which really pisses me off."

"How dreadful is that?"

"Auntie went through all of her funds in the nursing home and had to go on aid. But that's another story. You didn't come here to talk about my aunt. So, why are you here?"

"I felt badly about how we left things yesterday. We got off on the wrong foot. I wanted to reassure you BKC Properties has the utmost integrity. We'll work with you until we reach a comfortable solution for all parties."

"While I appreciate your efforts, I'm not concerned about a *comfortable solution*. This is my home; it will always be here for my offspring and their children. I'm sure you can understand my attachment. You've no idea what this represents in my life right now. I'm sure your high-powered attorneys will get you squared away with the town and get your pittance back." The tone in her voice elevated during the conversation, echoing through the empty house.

The rap on the open front door startled her.

"Kelli, you in here?" the masculine voice called out.

"Yes, we're in here, Gregg."

Officer Scott strutted into the messy dining area, his heavy boots scraping against the wood. "Thought I'd better check and see how you're doin'. How's that lump on the side of your head? Oh, I'm sorry. I didn't know you had company. Shit, Kesson, what're you doing here?"

"How nice to see you again. Officer Scott, I believe?"

"You believe, my ass. You know who I am, and I certainly know who you are. I would've thought you'd left town by now, looking for new land to ruin."

"For an officer of the law, you don't have an overabundance of friendly demeanor, do you?"

"My demeanor is fine. It all depends on who I'm addressing and how highly I think of them. In your case, you don't even rank."

The bickering irritated her. "Excuse me, you two," she interjected, "but I believe Officer Scott is here to see me, not have a discussion of how much he dislikes your projects, Rod."

Gregg had smoked as a teenager. His cough was deep-rooted. Had a lifetime of smoking caught up with him? He patted his pants pocket. She guessed he was searching for an inhaler.

"Kelli, can I talk to you privately, please?" Gregg asked.

"Sure—why don't we step into the room behind the front parlor. Excuse us, Rod. You know how to let yourself out."

"No problem here. I'll just look around."

She had hoped Rod would take the hint and leave, but he appeared bull headed and domineering, which irritated her further. But, why did part of her want him to stay?

The wallpaper on the walls of the room behind the front right parlor had peeled and exposed wooden slats with old horse hair insulation. Rusty hinges creaked on the nine-foot solid wood door when Gregg closed it.

He leaned against the hand-carved mantel. His elbow stirred up dust and almost knocked an antique oil lamp into the aged cracked mirror propped above the grand wood fireplace. She remembered well his exceptional coordination.

He cleared his raspy throat. "Sorry about that, Kelli. This asshole southern boy has bought property up and down the East Coast for the last couple of years. He doesn't give a shit 'bout history, preservation, or anything of importance. All he cares 'bout is making the big buck. When I heard what was going on, it ate right down to my gut, or what's left of it." He hacked again. "Stopped to see how you're doing after the other night."

"It's been a crazy couple of days. I'm doing okay physically, other than terrible headaches and a little vertigo, but more than that, I'm anxious to know what happened. I don't remember anything other than when I woke, with a gash on the side of my head and surrounded by hospital staff. Totally disoriented, I didn't know where I was. I kind of remember someone helped me to the street where I passed out and that makes no sense."

"Well, sweetie, strange things happen when you get hit on the head. Even with this tough noggin I've got, I've seen my share of stars, let me tell you," he joked.

"I don't know how to explain it. It was the most bizarre feeling I've ever had. And I didn't remember, at first, but bits and pieces are coming back a little at a time."

"Maybe Belinda Eldridge?" Gregg joked, his large belly jiggled.

She'd never shared with anyone except Aunt Hattie, but she was sure she'd seen Belinda numerous times when she had visited over the years. She believed in spirits and had always been curious by Auntie's stories.

After Steve died, there were several occasions where a sliver of hair showed up where she'd just cleaned. The Christmas morning the year after he died, a pristine white feather appeared on her pillow.

"Sorry to break up your party, but I've got an appointment in Boston, so I'm going to have to leave," Rod announced.

Startled by his appearance, they stopped their conversation.

"I assure you, Kelli, we'll have this matter resolved within a few days," Rod announced.

"As far as I'm concerned, it's already settled and starting today, I'm getting my ducks in a row and moving forward not only with the house—but my life too."

"You're leaving town?" Rod asked.

Was that an attempt at a bad joke? Is he an asshole or just trying to be cute?

"Not on your life, buster. Stop by anytime and see how the renovations are coming along," she boasted while her gut constricted.

Part of her wanted to see him again soon, while the other part hated this man and wished he would just go away.

CHAPTER 6

Gregg surveyed the mansion from his cruiser. It wasn't the mansion he thought of. He glanced at his cell phone he'd turned off to ensure no calls interrupted his chat with Kelli.

Kelli Goddard, his first love. And now she was back in town and a widow to boot. Was he still attracted to her after all these years?

As a teenager, she frustrated him like no other. Except the one he married who divorced him after three years to run off with an old fart with money and higher social status. Women. Who needed them? But, he had to admit, he always had a sweet spot for Kelli. She was still cute as a button.

He tapped the dashboard and drifted back in time.

The first time he truly noticed her as the opposite sex was twelve. His mother, God rest her soul, was good friends with Hattie. Kelli was invited to his birthday party which was held on Manomet Beach, his favorite place growing up. His father's friend had a ski boat and took the kids tubing which turned him into a superstar for the day.

He'd never forget how she looked in the pink two-piece bathing suit with multiple strings covered by a white oversized tee shirt, long auburn hair in a ponytail, skin tanned to golden perfection. Her body had filled out in all the right places which caused his hormones to kick into high gear whenever she slipped off the cover up that exposed taut small nipples through the fabric.

His family couldn't afford a house, so they rented one across the street from Hattie's. Surrounded by mature trees and foliage, they still had a partial view of the bay. His father had worked his way up the ranks of the police department, but part of his wages were spent on alcohol, gambling, or women. Even though his mother tried to hide his father's vices, he was old enough to know what the man did on the side.

He'd run into Kelli on the beach or occasionally bump into her at Gellar's Snackbar on State Road.

One of his passionate memories was when he was fourteen and participated in a kid's summer workshop at Priscilla Beach Theatre, a local haven for performing arts.

The original barn theatre on Rocky Hill Road had been closed for years, its box office boarded up and colorful doors locked. But that didn't prevent the owners from ongoing theatrical productions under a white large tent during the summer.

One of the thrills of the workshop was they got to view the inside balcony and theatre-style seats which led up to the stage where lights dangled dangerously. The theatre had quite the history of budding artists who had learned and performed, eventually making it big in theatre or movies.

The summer production was *Romeo and Juliet*. He'd never forget his part. Kelli was graced with the role of Juliet, so when he was designated the role of Romeo, it was perfect since he was smitten with Kelli.

A local philanthropist had donated used clothing for most of the productions, some from her own wardrobe back in the day. While he wasn't thrilled with his Shakespearean costume of velvet accented with gold embroidery, he enjoyed his crucial role portraying a rich nobleman.

Kelli wore a white taffeta layered over the royal blue satin gown, with a matching hat, white gloves, elaborate lace collar, and flat shoes.

The performance was well attended by relatives of the local children. There was a time when well-known actors were in town the line from the box office stretched all the way down the long driveway to Rocky Hill Road.

He wasn't a natural, but worked hard because he wanted to impress Kelli and get a chance to kiss her, which was the moment he cherished. It was known amongst local teenagers after that they were an item when Kelli visited each summer. From sunrise to sunset they were together on the beach. They fished, frolicked in the cold water, and climbed on wet, slippery jetty rocks covered in seaweed.

He helped Kelli collect sea glass which she displayed in a three-foot narrow jar in Hattie's bathroom. Fully intact shells were harder to find since most were broken by the time they reached the rocky shore. They strolled for hours and searched for clay pipes that would occasionally wash up from the White Star Lines' ship that hit the Mary Ann rocks and sunk off Stage Point decades ago.

Kelli's appearance on the front porch brought him back from daydreaming. He quickly started the car and drove away. He stared at her in his mirror and ran over the curb on his way out.

Maybe I'll luck out this time and be the man she's looking for. Think I'll have a Sam beer and work out tonight.

CHAPTER 7

Relieved Gregg and Rod had left, Kelli sat in a worn lawn chair on the unruly front yard under the hundred-year-old Gingko tree and surveyed the mansion. How could she have such conflicting feelings for these two men, one she'd known a long time and the other she didn't know at all? But her conflicts didn't stop there. The feelings about the old house baffled her too.

The house had decayed; cornices and fascia boards were missing. No wonder the structure leaked with shingles absent and cracked. There were only two chimneys. Hadn't there once been three?

Multiple siding boards were gone, but wood brackets and modillions below the soffits seemed in good condition. While the windows and French doors appeared to be in fair shape, the window sills definitely would have to be replaced.

It broke her heart her favorite wrap-around porches had crumbled to pieces, especially where a brush burning had caught the north side. She prayed portions of the canopy and decorative brackets could be salvaged.

Good Lord—what have I gotten myself into? There's no way in hell I can restore this house. Why did you leave it to me, Auntie? Why didn't you gift it to the historical society like we talked about?

Her passion was unrivaled for this house and land, naturally drawn to them since a young child. It was mystical. Wonderful memories over the years made an even stronger connection than she realized.

She closed her eyes; her head rested on metal. The heat of the sun bore down on her wearied body. She drifted back to when she was eight.

The gargantuan mansion had overwhelmed her, but her aunt's loving touches made her feel at home and always loved.

When her feet hit the steps on the arched wrap-around porch, aromas of fresh baked pies, pastries, and boiled lobster wafted past her. Jovial laughter and her aunt's beefy arms squeezed hard enough to almost smother her in the large breasts. She giggled at the image of the wrinkled cleavage.

Rainy days or sunny skies, they spent hours on the covered porch ordained with overflowing ferns, pastel impatiens, and peach-colored double geraniums. Off-white wicker furniture sat around the sides along with Auntie's collection of anchors, sea shells, buoys, driftwood, and other treasures collected from a lifetime of living by the sea.

Auntie was big-boned and stood six-foot-three. No one dared upset her apple cart. Anything a man could do, Auntie could do better. She rarely indulged in make-up or fluffed her shoulder-length fine hair, which gave a thinned, stringy appearance.

Even though Auntie never married, a local fisherman, Captain Maz, was her long-time friend and cohort. She suspected they'd done some hanky-panky by the way they touched and spoofed each other.

Captain Maz was a kind, bear of a gentle man. Truly a vision of the old man in the sea. His tanned leather skin exhibited years that had been bestowed by the elements. Each deep crease told a story. Shiny white thick hair to his shoulders was his trademark and could be identified from a distance on his boat if a hat had blown off. The benevolence and gentleness he bestowed on humans and animals endeared him to all that knew him. Made of grandfather material, he never had a chance since he didn't marry. After all, he had Hattie.

A large leaf from the tree startled her when it flitted onto her face. Her right arthritic knee had stiffened, so she sauntered to the bluff to loosen her body before she started physical labor inside the house. The renters had left one hell of a mess for her to clean up.

The estate was magnificent beyond words, even after all these years. Packed with mature cedars, maples, oaks, and horse chestnuts, the aged trees shed broken limbs and debris but they all seemed healthy just neglected. It still served as a canopy which allowed streams of sunlight through, cooling the land on hot days, yet stabilizing the soil on the bluff.

The wind, soft as a cotton puff, grazed her body while she made the trek. Wild rosa rugosa, wisteria, and honeysuckle filled the air with sweetness and reminded her of aromas from freshly steamed tea.

She stumbled over a piece of rusted wrought iron and almost tumbled to the ground. Was it a section of an old fence that was part of the cemetery Auntie had told her about? According to information passed down from generations, Captain Eldridge buried family members on the estate, but no one knew for sure where since overgrown foliage consumed the area.

Her mind drifted. Manomet was their family summer vacation destination. Living in the Midwest, the most exciting activity in summertime and fall was the community swimming pool, Oktoberfest, and when farmers harvested grain and corn. Her family kept a small garden full of sweet corn, cucumbers, tomato plants, and green peppers and she'd learned how to can bread and butter pickles.

Her parents, James and Karen Greene, were middle class folks, her dad a manager at a local grocery store, her mom a secretary at an elementary school.

The annual car trip required two days out and back and was a huge event for their family of four. Her father only received two weeks' vacation annually and her mother didn't work at the school during the summer break, but coached autistic children from home.

She idealized her brother Blake, a year older. They had grown up close in age, so he took her under his wing and protected her if anyone looked at her crossways. His general sense of kindness to all was what she admired about him the most.

He worked hard during the summers and detasseled corn. He saved his money for his first car, his pride and joy, a fast and flashy sixty-nine orange and white striped Camaro. She was honored to be the first passenger to ride around the town loop.

A month after he turned sixteen, he was involved in a head-on collision with a drunk driver. He perished instantly. It was the worst day of her life—until the day her husband died.

Overwhelming dread and depression consumed her often and when it did, the one comfort that brought back some sense of normalcy was fond memories of their summers in Manomet.

Her dad had purchased a used sixty-six Ford station wagon with a rear facing seat. She'd fought with Blake over the back seat and while he pretended to put up a good fight, she always won because he allowed it. Besides, it was furthest from her dad's cigarette smoke. God, she hated that smell. It was hard to breathe if she sat up front.

Packing journal, books, pillow, and blanket, she slept most of the way since she suffered from travel sickness. Once the car moved, she was out like a light. That was probably why Blake conceded on the back seat issue. The trip was long and tedious; her parents took turns driving during the earlier years.

After Blake died, everything changed. Her parents barely spoke to each other. The house was filled with an uneasy silence. They seemed to blame each other for his death, but neither had a role. It was an unbearable time for all. The tension in the house caused her to find any excuse to stay away from home. She stayed out late and found solace in being wild with her friends.

But worse—something transpired between her mom and Auntie shortly after Blake's death. Numerous times she overheard her mother and Hattie on the phone. From her mother's end, the conversation was heated. When she tried to eavesdrop, she couldn't hear clearly. But the gist of it was her mother no longer wanted to visit Manomet. It was a topic her parents wouldn't discuss with her no matter how many times she pressed for an explanation.

The summer after Blake's death, her mother finally agreed to fly her to Providence where Hattie picked her up. She was allowed to stay the entire summer, just her and Auntie. Truth was, it was a relief to be away from the sadness that had consumed her parents and home.

Her heart lightened with memories of Auntie whose love abounded. Since Auntie had never married, she became her child of sorts with new adventures with every trip.

Clothes rustic, khakis with oversized sweatshirt or tee-shirt was Auntie's style, more often than not without a bra. The only time she wore a dress was to funerals. Would her breasts sag and crease like Auntie's? She hoped not since she had not followed the woman's style.

But she loved everything about the mansion. Since the house sat on the bluff, the view from every window was awe-inspiring, even when the oak trees grew taller and blocked some of the panorama. It was so different from Broward which was nothing but flat land, cornfields, and soybeans for miles. But Broward was home. While it was a little town, it did have some celebrity with a local resident turned author who published *Uncharted Depths* and *The Apparition*, novels with local roots, a true mystery, and intrigue.

Over years of visits she became a strong swimmer, eventually allowed on Auntie's lobster skiff to help pull lobster pots. She'd never forget her first trip out on *Tinker Belle*, Auntie's catboat, to troll for bait for the lobster pots around the Mary Ann Rocks. The following day they prepped to make sure they had enough bait bags. They hauled stinky totes of bait down the long stairs to the beach.

The dinghy was stored upside down next to the rocks on the bluff. Hattie dragged it to the shoreline where they climbed in and rowed to the mooring where the work boat sat. After a clumsy transfer, Auntie surprised her and pulled out a brand new set of rubber gloves and bib, an early birthday gift. They donned their attire to protect from gross crud and cold water when they hauled up the traps, but more importantly, to ward off the relentless grip of lobster and rock crab claws which latched onto their bare hands.

At first, she was inept when she pulled creatures from the nets and placed the rancid bait inside the traps, but became more accustomed to the routine each time they went out. She loved being with her aunt on the open water. There were no worries, no sadness—just freedom.

Lobsters, crab, striped bass, flounder, cod, haddock, tautog, fluke, and steamed clams were mainstays for dinner and so was Captain Maz. Over time, he became a pseudo uncle. She'd occasionally catch a glimpse of him giving Auntie a peck on the cheek or a squeeze on her behind.

Why didn't they marry? When older, she asked Auntie.

"Why fix something that's not broke, honey. Things work just fine the way we are."

When she reached the bluff, she took a deep breath and exhaled. She raised her arms above her head and absorbed the beauty of the ocean. It was resplendent, regardless of how many times she viewed it, always different, beautiful stormy or calm.

Eighty-feet above sea level, the little community painted an astonishing landscape of calm water, sailboats, and tenders fastened to weathered white buoys; colored buoys represented lobster pots that dangled below. Cobalt water complemented the powder-blue sky while patches of seaweed produced shaded dimensions.

It was a typical summer day on the bay. Lobster pots were checked; fishermen scurried from one buoy to the next. Kids darted and hollered. They threw balls and

Frisbees, some chased by barking dogs. Families grilled hot dogs and hamburgers which filled the air with delectable aromas.

Multi-colored umbrellas or tents provided shade on the coarse sandy beach while a yellow sailboat with green and white striped sails skimmed the water close to shore. Red and blue kayaks perched off Stage Point, likely scoping out grunting seals.

When the brisk wind switched from the north, the distinct odor of rotted seaweed and tangled crabs wafted up the bluff. Winter storms had been brutal. It saddened her the bottom portion of the wooden beach stairs had been replaced with metal steps by one of the neighbors.

This was how life was supposed to be—peaceful, serene, nature at its finest. Everyone brimmed with love, happiness, and gratitude for an incredible day God had bestowed.

Why am I melancholy on such a beautiful day?

Her life had almost been perfect until five years ago when she lost her soul mate, the love of her life, her best friend and husband of twenty-eight years. In seconds, her idealistic life was shattered.

She positioned herself close to the bluff on the moist grass, not concerned if stains appeared on her old jean shorts. Her soul ached for so many reasons. Her husband was dead; he'd left her emotionally and financially bankrupt, and angered with his lies.

Her auntie's wish for her to salvage the mansion was going to cost millions—unrealistic by any stretch. Auntie made a statement the last time she visited, over and over like a broken record. The mansion held secrets. She wondered if the Alzheimer's had eaten away at the dear old woman's brain then.

"I will help you," a meek voice whispered.

Jarred by the voice, she turned in all directions. She was the only person on the bluff.

CHAPTER 8

Well-known locally as rabble rousers, Bubba Smithe and Johnny Roberts sat on uneven wooden bar stools they claimed daily after working at the fish market in Plymouth. They never showered before their self-induced happy hour, thus forcing other patrons to crowd the opposite end of the bar if they weren't in the same physical state.

Bubba smiled. Their reputation preceded them. Friends since childhood, he and Johnny had been in trouble with the law since young boys, thirteen to be exact. Thank goodness, Gregg's dad, the police chief, had gone to school with their fathers and got them off the hook more than the officer would ever admit.

"So, did ya hear about the new chick in town?" Bubba inquired of Johnny.

"Yeah, heard someone attacked the lady at the mansion," Johnny blared out. He glanced over his shoulder at the small crowd.

"Why'd ya suppose someone would attack her? That ole' dilapidated place has nothin' in it, other than a lot of myths and maybe a ghost or two," he joked. "Ya know, the fellas at the fishery yack their jaws about ole' Sea Captain Eldridge hiding all that loot in that gone to ruin place," Bubba explained. "Overheard one feller say some construction company paid mega bucks for the property 'cause they believe when they yank 'er down, they'll find rare coins probably worth millions now. Maybe I'll switch jobs and work for 'em. Ain't making no money fuckin' rippin' up these stinky fish six days a week."

"Ya know, Bubba, sometimes I think ya've jus' gone wicked crazy thinkin' ya're gonna get rich for nothin'. Jus' plum nuts."

"Fuck you, Johnny. You guys will be the laughingstock when I do. Well, look who the chowder heads drug in. How ya doing there, ole' Scottie boy?"

"Doing well. And what are you two losers up to today?" Gregg inquired.

"Now is that any way to talk to ya buddies? Jus' hanging," Bubba replied. "What's the scoop on the new babe in town gettin' smacked at the mansion the other night? What the hell's up with that?"

Gregg raised his hand to get the attention from the bartender who didn't ask for his order.

"Attacked? Well, we're not sure about that. Still trying to put together pieces of that evening. She doesn't remember anything." He glanced at Johnny, their unkempt eyebrows hiked in unison.

"Also heard you and that lady used to be an item at one time," Johnny teased.

"Item we weren't. Friends, yeah. Back in the day we ran around together when she visited Hattie in the summer."

"People are talkin'. Guess her gettin' attacked has refueled ole' rumors of the mansion having coins hidden by wacked out Captain Eldridge," Johnny added.

"You boys still listening to rumors? You oughta know by now living here all your life. It's nothing but gossip. No one's ever found a coin in that place and never will. You boys need to quit dreaming and keep working hard," Gregg reprimanded loudly, causing patrons to eavesdrop on their conversation. "You're not getting any freebies in this lifetime."

"Look who's talkin'. Shit, you townie. Ya were handed your job on a silver platter only 'cause of your pop, so ya sure as hell don't have any room to grunt 'bout us bein' losers," he replied. "If my papa had handed me anything, maybe things would've turned out differently. All I had was a drunkard who didn't know which ass side was up and beat us kids." Instantly, he regretted that statement.

Bubba's bi-polar depression had hit an all-time low that day for some unknown reason. He contemplated walking out of work, claiming he was sick, but looked forward to their daily happy hour which usually lifted his spirits, even if he got sick of Johnny day after day. Seemed like drinking was about the only happy thing in his life right now.

It depressed him when he glanced around the bar. Every day it was the same group of men who smelled of fish, beer, butts, and cigars. They cussed enough to warrant a sailor back to sea and whistled at new blood that walked in on rare occasions.

He should've left town when he had the chance. After several operating under the influence charges and possibly facing jail time, his uncle in Boston was sympathetic and offered a job at his machine shop, but he declined. Probably the biggest mistake of his life, other than when he should have stood up to his father and his heathen ways. He'd never be anything better than a slave to a bunch of fish.

"So, Scottie...how're things down at the department?" Johnny asked.

"Pretty slow considering the time of year. Lots of traffic accidents off Plimoth Plantation Highway and Route Three with people making their way to the Cape. After all these years, you'd think they'd come up with a plan so they don't have to sit in traffic for hours at a time. Most tourists come once a year, so they don't know where the hell they're going." Gregg chugged his beer. "More OUI's than usual off White Horse Beach plus a lot of illegal parking. Never ceases to amaze me they can make their way up from the beach to even get in their vehicles."

"Heard ya've had idiots that got too close to the nuclear plant. What in the hell are they thinkin'?" Bubba inquired.

"Not locals. Usually seasonal renters on the Cape. They don't know the restrictions for the power plant. Seems to me if you're going to rent out a cottage, the owners should inform them what they can and cannot do, especially if you're taking out a boat you're not familiar with and don't know the area." He nodded at the bartender for another drink. "Can't tell you how many people lose props on the rocks when the tide is high. Damn flatlanders. But, that's how it goes around here. SDSS—same day, same shit," Gregg remarked, a disgruntled tone in his voice.

The men sucked down three more drinks and whittled away a couple of hours at the bar.

"That's enough for me, boys. Think I'll head home," Gregg announced.

"Yeah, we're not far behind ya," Johnny replied.

"See ya guys tomorrow." Gregg waved and walked out the door.

"Fuckin' idiot." He slid off the bar stool. "Let's go, Johnny. We've got plans to make."

CHAPTER 9

"*Hey, Troy. Do me a favor. I want to know everything* about Kelli Goddard, Hattie Hubbard, the Manomet Mansion ASAP," Rod requested. He surveyed the bay from the back of the yacht.

What was there about this woman that intrigued him? He rarely paid any attention to a connection between him and a woman this quickly; they hadn't even touched. She was different from any female he'd ever met, especially in his society circles.

Her skin was radiant with minimal wrinkles for a woman her age and she appeared to not wear much make-up. Her naturally pink, moist lips caught his attention. She threw out rapid words, probably an educated woman.

Softness in her aquamarine eyes and ability to maintain constant eye contact added to her appeal, but there were hints she was sad and stressed. Her jewelry was quaint and tasteful; loose-fitted clothes complemented her firm and toned body, but truthfully, he could only make that judgment if she were unclothed.

Her attitude is anything other than casual. He laughed.

How well known was she around town? How much public support could she gain if she put up a fight? His investigators would leave no stone unturned.

Life is Good, the name of his yacht, was tied to the last dock at Brewers Boat Yard in Plymouth Bay. He had grown fond of this area since his short stay. The boardwalk had a security gate, so no one could pass through and gain access to his boat, plus his crew never left it unattended. An ocean craft of this magnitude caught the eye of the curious, vandals, and thieves.

The water was the calmest he'd seen in a while. The captain had instructions to cruise far enough he could view the tip of P'town. He didn't feel like being around anyone tonight since he was in one of his introvert moods.

With manicured bare tan feet propped on the shellacked hand-crafted wooden table, he opened the binder hand delivered from the local private investigator. He was amazed the man had accumulated the information in such a short period of time.

Several hours of daylight were left before sunset, his favorite time of day. The white, three-ring binder had been professionally prepared. Tabs indicated: *Kelli Goddard, Hattie Hubbard, Manomet Mansion.*

He flipped to Kelli Goddard's tab and sipped on Grey Goose vodka, swished fresh lemons around the ice cubes. He quickly scanned personal information highlighted in yellow.

> **...Midwestern woman, born and raised in Broward, Illinois.**
> **...Forty-seven on July third.**

Oh dear, nearly menopausal. Shit, no wonder she's a firecracker. He laughed out loud at his terrible sense of humor.

> **...Parents deceased.**
> **...Brother deceased at age sixteen.**
> **...One son, Rick, in Indiana and two granddaughters, ages four and six.**

...BS from the University of Illinois in childhood behavior.

...Widowed five years.

...Husband died in single car accident. A financial advisor involved in Ponzi scheme discovered after his death. Caused her to file bankruptcy. Bank repossessed all assets.

...Personal notes: Taught developmentally challenged children with autism, master gardener, civically involved, loved animals. Doting mother and grandmother.

His father might actually approve of a woman of her stature even though he also seemed to prefer attractive bimbos with big tits and no brains who flirted with him. His mother would adore this woman who was more like her southern relatives, down to earth, service before self.

And why would I care if my parents approved of her? They'd given up on him settling down and providing them with grandchildren.

He picked out an expensive Edicion Limigtada Cuban cigar from the humidor and attempted to light it. The breeze made it difficult. The aroma lingered around his head.

...Hattie Hubbard. Died three years ago at age seventy-nine from complications from advanced stage Alzheimer's and MS. Resided in Glen Ellen Nursing Home seven years.

Wow—no wonder the mansion had been so neglected. Why didn't someone in her family take care of it?

…Bequeathed only asset, her residence, to niece, Kelli Goddard. Other family members were excluded in the will.

…Ms. Hubbard, one of the few native residents of Manomet, was well known for rescuing stray animals, injured birds, and occasionally baby seals. Naturalist and green before green was cool. Cared deeply about her town and community, actively supporting it .

…Member of the Tidmarsh Farms Restoration Project, a sanctuary where acres of cranberry bogs were being returned to their natural wetlands .

…Homelessness was one of her causes which upset local residents. She'd occasionally take in strangers during the brutal winter months.

…Grew organic gardens and donated food to local shelters and food pantries.

It appeared from several attached articles Ms. Hubbard was a woman with the strength not to buckle under political or local pressures and fought for her beliefs.

The next tab was labeled *The Manomet Mansion*. He didn't see any purpose of reviewing the file since he'd perused the reports before he purchased the property.

Relighting the large cigar was difficult since the breeze stirred, but once he did, smooth smoke created a cloud of its own. He momentarily forgot what he was doing. His mind wandered while chattering white sea gulls glided effortlessly above, searching for food below the water.

He closed his eyes and relieved the tension in his shoulders. The breeze flowed over his face; heat of the setting sun penetrated his skin. The waves splashed against the hull which almost lulled him to sleep.

He loathed his job some days but had no right to complain, or so his father convinced him when he was a young man. From the time he walked before one, his father encouraged him to be tough and excel at everything he attempted.

He wasn't supposed to cry when he fell or broke a bone in his arm from football. If someone hit him, smack them back five times harder. If they outperformed him in a sport, his father hired the best trainers. No one upstaged a Kesson.

He always had to be the winner, regardless of what he did. If he wasn't, it was the ultimate disappointment for his father, who belittled him as a form of discipline.

How many times had he dreamed of running away to escape this pressure and shove the money and business up his father's ass? How often had he contemplated sailing his yacht around the world with no contact, especially with his father?

One of the main reasons he hadn't walked away from the business was his mother, bless her sweet soul. She tried through the years to support him and keep peace in the family, although difficult at times with his father's stubbornness and unrelenting ways.

His thoughts were interrupted when the steward, Sy, handed him the cell phone.

"Sorry, sir. I know you didn't want to be disturbed, but your father insisted."

He took a huge puff. He hesitated then answered. "Yes, Father. What can I do for you?"

"Tell me the rumor I just heard isn't true. Ya've got issues with the mansion up there?" his father questioned in a familiar harsh tone, southern drawl strong and loud.

"Yep—we've got issues. But according to Troy, we dotted our i's and crossed our t's, so should be a matter for the title company who's going to have to delve into the records."

"You know how important this condominium project is, so I'm sure ya're all over it. Right?"

"Yep, have it under control." He hated when his father spoke in a condescending tone, constantly micro managing.

"I've heard that before, Rodney. I'll expect a full report tomorrow from ya and Troy. Board meeting is next week and enormous amounts of money are at stake. And our reputation."

"Father, it's under control," he acknowledged, his voice firm.

"Well, make sure it is."

The phone clicked in his ear.

He massaged his neck while his abdominals pinched in pain. Why did he allow his father to get to him like that? After all, he wasn't a little boy to be controlled anymore. When would he stop needing his father's approval?

His calm day had been ruined. The wind increased and blew out his cigar. The vodka was gone. To hell with it. He might go back into town and see what was happening at the mansion. Maybe she'd heard from her attorney.

I've already had one ass chewing. Maybe I'll go get another from the interesting lady. Maybe I enjoy it in some masochistic sort of way. I do like a woman with spunk.

CHAPTER 10

Kelli positioned herself on the warped board on the front porch and picked at her chipped shellac nail polish. She had really let herself go since her husband died. She sighed. She had little interest in how she looked anymore.

Her nervous stomach roiled as she gazed at the overrun clusters of evergreen shrubs, deciduous hedgerow, and invasive bittersweet. Uneven mounds of dirt and weeds were knee high. The feeling was similar to when she'd eat a meal late at night. Acid reflux would flare up, burning her throat as it traversed her esophagus. The taste was vile.

No wonder newcomers to Manomet had no idea the mansion existed since the hedgerow blocked the view from the road. The narrow driveway was the only indication something existed beyond the barrier of plants.

Another morning of sunniness was the only redeeming factor so far. What was she going to do? How would she sort out this entire mess? Not only the mansion, but her personal life too.

Tears streamed down her cheek. How could she recover from her husband's death and accept he left her in financial ruin? Why hadn't he confided in her? After almost thirty years of marriage, didn't they trust each other? Or, had he tried to protect her? Was there another woman? Gambling problem?

She wasn't ignorant about finances. She had a college degree, but he insisted on not only paying bills, but prepared financial statements and tax returns. She insisted they maintain separate checking accounts which allowed her independence.

Come to think of it, have I ever signed a tax return?

According to her attorney, a mutual friend since high school, no financial assets remained except for the house which was held jointly. The hefty mortgage and home equity line of credit wiped out all equity.

Early in their marriage they struggled emotionally and financially while Steve built up his business. She juggled work, volunteered, and raised a family. There were plenty of amazing memories and lots of dreams. With a blink of the eye, they vanished.

She was undeniably in love the first time she spotted her soul mate at a local donut shop where she waited tables at sixteen.

Coal black shiny hair just above his shoulders caught her attention. He was the most handsome guy she'd ever seen. She was instantly attracted, not only because of looks, but to his carefree attitude and love of life.

Two spirits connected once they were introduced by mutual friends. While they dated off and on for several years, in her heart she knew they'd be together until death-do-us part. The death part came sooner than she expected.

High school sweethearts, they married shortly after graduation. They lived a simple and fulfilled life. She was a secretary and helped children with autism while he attended college and obtained a degree in finance.

She later attended community college and obtained an associates in child behavior. After three years of marriage and scrimping to save, they bought their dream home, an old country two-story house located on the outskirts of the small farming community. The following year they were blessed with the most precious gift, a son. She worked from home where she tutored children until their son was in second grade, then returned to college and got her bachelor's degree.

All her dreams had come true. The house with the white picket fence, a soul mate, healthy and beautiful child, and a black lab, Wags. Years flew. While there were valleys in their marriage, they were a close family and enjoyed traveling to Disneyland, camping, and fishing.

Steve's business thrived in the community of two thousand, mostly farmers. It was easy to procure business because everyone in town trusted him. His father had been the president of the local bank and, while he didn't want to follow in his professional footsteps, he chose to build his own business.

With his father's financial assistance, he expanded to a larger city thirty miles away. They borrowed money and hated to be more in debt, but it proved to be a prudent business decision.

That seemed to be the turning point in the downhill decline in their marriage. Business kept him away from home overnight, and he often traveled to Chicago, St. Louis, or Indianapolis. She was never invited, which became a bone of contention between them.

His easy-going attitude switched to temperamental, easily upset at minor situations. Normally, when she purchased items, it was at her discretion. She worked at school in the special education department which provided her spending money.

Their last fight was over a coat she'd purchased. Costs were controlled with their son at college. So—she splurged. When she mentioned she'd spent five hundred on a coat, Steve went on a rampage and stomped around the house. He shattered a lamp, something he'd never done in almost three decades of marriage. He rushed angrily out of the house and didn't come home that night. Worried out of her mind, she called his cell all night and left voice mails while she paced until the sole of her slipper tore.

It was six the next morning when the doorbell rang. Troy and Jim, local officers and friends, stood at the door. Something terribly tragic had happened. Her heart skipped beats. Was it Steve?

She'd never forget Troy's words.

"Kelli, let's go sit down. I have some...bad news." Those two words would be burned into her brain forever.

"There's been a car accident. Steve didn't make it," Troy announced and grabbed her hand.

They said she collapsed and fell off the chair. The next thing she recalled Troy, Jim, and several neighbors stood over her while flat on her back, a strong odor was forced into her face.

Steve dead? Her beloved husband gone forever? Not possible. There had to be a mistake. The good weren't supposed to die young. An accident? How would she tell this devastating news to their son? His father had been his best friend. Their family unit would be shattered. She couldn't fathom living a day without him.

According to the state police, he died instantly. On his way back from Bloomington, a town forty miles northwest, from a business meeting, a large buck jumped out from a growth of trees and underbrush and into the middle of Interstate 74.

The police said there was no way he could've avoided the large animal. He hit the animal head on, lost control of his BMW, and slid down an embankment until it plunged into a shallow lake.

The car behind witnessed the accident and stopped. The elderly and frail gentleman attempted to reach Steve while the car sank, but it filled with water too quickly. The autopsy showed Steve was dead from head and internal injuries before he hit the water. If he hadn't, he would've drowned.

She replayed over and over how his last minutes might have been. It was important to her to know if he suffered. If he was not unconscious, was he scared? The thought of him feeling pain or worse, being fearful, caused her legs to ache.

The days before and after the funeral were a blur. She moved in slow motion and took care of business and was constantly surrounded by family and friends. Her concern was her son's welfare and focused any leftover energy on him.

The hardest time, other than the funeral, was the day everyone went back to their daily lives. She realized she didn't have a normal anymore. The big house was eerily quiet. It didn't make any difference what she had for dinner. There was no one to cook for.

Normally, she would have sat on the couch with the television on and waited for the door to open. Her husband would plunk down his briefcase on the kitchen counter, car keys jingled. The silence now was eerie. She missed his tight hug and passionate kiss after a hard day at work.

With the help of friends who were in the financial and legal professions, she faced one of the largest tasks. The estate. She had little knowledge of their money matters since Steve had taken care of the finances.

While they made a point to discuss major purchases, she trusted her husband to take care of everything.

A week after the funeral, she delved into sorting out paperwork and files. She cussed at him for the terrible shape he'd left the office in, papers everywhere and in no particular order. But more for dying.

She couldn't believe what she found. While he verbally kept her abreast of the accounts, where they were and balances, she hadn't actually seen a statement in decades. She trusted Steve with everything, her life, love, and future.

The paperwork confused her. She tried to make sense of the balances. The joint checking account at the local bank down the street had less than five-hundred dollars. His last retirement statement showed less than a thousand. There had to be an error. According to Steve, he contributed the maximum to both of their IRA's and retirement accounts, which should have been hundreds of thousands of dollars by now.

A stack of notices from the mortgage company and local bank where they'd financed two new cars and Rinker Cuddy Cabin were in a yellow envelope under the pile. Past due; all the statements indicated past due. Letters referenced they were in the process of being turned over to collection agencies.

A gut-wrenched knot filled her stomach when she recalled that day. After numerous meetings with her attorney, they discovered he'd borrowed against and depleted every financial asset, home equity, and line of credit.

Had he kept a mistress? What had he done with the money, over a million dollars?

She combed through statement after statement for days. He'd developed a clever and underhanded scheme. He'd secured investors and formed one partnership after the other. Funds from the new partnerships were being used to pay dividends, giving the owners outstanding returns which kept everyone happy. Fictitiously, he achieved incredible returns in down markets and was hailed a financial genius.

Basically, he borrowed from Peter to pay Paul. The attorney confirmed it was an elaborate Ponzi scheme. When funds became tight, he borrowed from their personal money to return dividends to investors.

In desperation, he used their funds for gambling, probably hoping to hit a big jackpot and clear him from the drowning debt and humiliation to his family and friends. It now crossed her mind that maybe the accident wasn't an accident after all? Maybe he could have avoided the deer but chose not to? But then he'd let all life insurance policies lapse.

Had he planned to tell her about their desperate situation? Would he have eventually confided in her and asked for help? They'd shared everything in their marriage, or so she thought.

What other secrets had he kept from her? She shook her shoulders. She prayed the hellish memories would vanish.

Focus on the positive now. The past is the past. Go forward.

Her precious gifts were her son, his wife, and two granddaughters. That's what she'd fight for, to pass the mansion, an anchor, the root of their ancestry, on to them and future generations—a second home for the granddaughters and their children to spend summers in

Manomet just like she had. To create memories and love.

Placing her family in the forefront boosted her spirits when depressed. Steve had not only died and abandoned her, but his dishonesty destroyed her trust in people in general. Had she been emotionally damaged beyond repair?

Ironic, isn't it?

The bank discreetly foreclosed on her home in Broward where everyone knew her business, but rented it back to her for a nominal fee until she could get on her feet. She inherited Auntie's mansion—and now some friggin' company wanted to take it away from her? She chuckled, not from happiness, but from the sheer irony of life's unfair hand.

Her backbone straightened. Whenever she was at her lowest, God had always given her an incredible gift of pulling herself up and going forward. Right now, she was isolated and alone, just like the day Steve died. Could she handle one more crisis?

Returned to reality by the churning of a diesel engine while it drove up the drive, her pulse accelerated. Rod Kesson was back. Deep down she was thrilled and intrigued, but all she needed today was him to harass her about possession of the mansion. It was the only asset she owned. Even though the house was in total ruination, the eighty acres was worth a king's ransom located on Cape Cod Bay. No one would take it from her. Especially him.

"Good morning, Kelli. How are you?"

"I'd be much better if you came to tell me your legal team has rectified the situation, and you have no right to my property," she acknowledged.

"Great way to start a conversation so early in the morning."

"Might as well get the facts on the table, don't you think?" She tried to make eye contact but couldn't through the expensive sunglasses.

His dark brown hair was shiny and glistened in the sun; slivers of gray framed the temples. Length was longer than she'd expect for a man his age, but fashionably cut and styled away from his square jaws, a European look. Well groomed and handsome, he was a man any woman would look at twice. If there was one thing a man could do to catch her attention, it would be to wear a sensual cologne, which he was.

His pressed olive shirt was tucked into well-tailored jeans. The outfit was complete with shiny brown boots and a small gold necklace which flickered in the sun's rays. His broad shoulders complemented a well-shaped waist. She assumed he spent a great deal of time at gyms. Most men his age showed excesses of life at their mid-section.

"Unfortunately, I have no news. My legal team is on it, but thought perhaps the two of us might be able to work this out."

"The two of us?" She attempted a nervous fake laugh.

"Mind if I sit and chat?"

She scooted over, careful not to pick up a sliver of distressed wood through her cut-off dungarees. "Doubt it will do any good, but go ahead."

He sat closer than she would have liked, but enjoyed it when his arm touched hers. A tide surged through her. He probably did it on purpose, hoping to force her blood pressure to rise.

"You know, if you continue to have this negative attitude, it's going to be tough to reach any type of compromise."

"Compromise? I'm telling you right now there will *not* be a compromise. This house means the world to me, to my family, my grandchildren. This is the only legacy I have left to give them. You don't understand what I've...." She tried not to burst out crying.

She rose and stepped into the parlor on the right side of the entrance doors where Rod couldn't see how distraught and vulnerable she was.

"I'm sorry. I didn't mean to upset you." He followed with soft steps while he surveyed the house.

"Upset? Who's upset?" She struggled with a heavy box.

"You appear upset to me? Here, let me help."

"Thanks, but I can do it myself. Look, my patience is running low this morning already, so I suggest we leave any compromise discussions to our attorneys. I'm really not the best company right now. Perhaps it'd be best if you leave."

"Sorry you feel that way. Most people would try to work towards a compromise. Guess that doesn't interest you? I'd be happy to stick around and give you a hand."

"Compromise, no that absolutely doesn't interest me. I'll tell you what does. I got up this morning and expected peace and quiet. Enjoy the morning sunshine and birds singing on my land. Call it reflection, meditation, or whatever. Things you probably have no idea about."

"Gracious. I apologize and if that's what you want I'll—"

"That's exactly what I want. Thanks for stopping by. I'm sorry. I'm not trying to be rude, I'm just...."

The thump of his heels on the wooden porch signaled he had exited. She gasped for air.

What is wrong with me? It is so against my nature to be rude. I am pushing him away.

The truck sped down the gravel road which spewed rocks into the weeds. She dropped to her knees and bawled uncontrollably. Coiled into a fetal position, she rocked back and forth on the dusty, worn rug.

I don't think I can do this.

A ripple of warmth lightly caressed her back which caused her shirt to shift up and down on her clammy skin.

"It's going to be okay. I will help you, but I need your help too," a voice whispered.

When she rolled to her back, she caught a glimpse of a translucent, lustrous red fabric gliding up the stairway.

CHAPTER 11

It took Kelli a while to regroup. She worried she might have *a* nervous breakdown. By early afternoon she'd made her overwhelming list and prioritized it. She focused on baby steps, one at a time. She had to remember to breathe and quit thinking about Rod Kesson.

If this house hadn't meant so much to Auntie, she'd let it remain with the town for back taxes. If BKC Properties bought it, that'd be none of her business.

As her aunt aged, she incessantly emphasized how important this land and house was not only to her, but imperative for future generations. She insinuated years before Alzheimer's struck the house held secrets no one but her knew, but the disease spread rapidly. She never divulged details.

When Auntie referred to the unknown, long natural eyelashes outlined her puffy, big brown eyes which were surrounded by skin that sagged around her neck, making wrinkles over her mouth.

Hats were her trademark and she always wore one outside. An old sailor's cap was her favorite. While it helped shield her face, years of exposure created deep-seated wrinkles. The brown spots she suspected were basal or squamous cell cancer, not that Auntie would ever go to a doctor to find out.

Auntie joked often, making it difficult to know when she was serious. Mysteries and truths were locked away in a brain destroyed by the debilitating disease. The last few times she visited, Hattie didn't recognize her. She incessantly called her Belinda. The nurses reported

Hattie had constant conversations with her make believe friend, Belinda.

Belinda like in Belinda Eldridge?

Whenever she had asked Auntie about ghosts and rumors of the mansion, her answer was routine—*spirits live on forever.* Then she hugged and kissed her. That was it.

Kelli strolled through the front parlor on the left which contained eight-foot bay windows and shared a fireplace with the dining room on the opposite end.

One of her favorite pieces in the house was a built-in china cabinet in the corner. Auntie displayed mismatched antique glass collected over decades. The arched cabinet reached the ceiling, designed to match the hobbit door in the corner of the hall. The cabinet was unique in design and handcrafted with wooden circles and x's placed above the smoky glass.

Obsessed with estate sales, Auntie collected small antiques to the point the cabinet overflowed. Her favorites were dainty china saucers with matching teacups, some over two-hundred years old.

On special occasions when she was young, Auntie pulled them out for a tea party on the front porch, complete with antique dolls and linen tablecloths. The tenants had either absconded or broken most of her collection, unaware of their value or sentimental worth.

When she swiped her finger across the first dusty wooden shelf, it caught on a note and small key taped to the underside of the second shelf. She pulled them off with ease, but the note was unreadable after all the years. She turned the key over in her hand. What did it open?

"Anybody home," a raspy voice called from the entrance. "Yes." She stepped off the unsteady stool and stuck the paper and key in her pocket.

"Well, I'll be damned, if it isn't that little sweetheart, Kelli Goddard," an old man announced. He hobbled into the room with cane in hand.

She recognized the voice immediately. "Oh, my God. Is that you, Captain Maz?"

"You can bet the house," he replied. "I'm still a kickin."

She darted across the room and enfolded his hunched-over shoulders in her arms and held him tightly; moisture filled her eyes. Through his rumpled tee shirt she could tell he wasn't beefy like the last time she saw him at Auntie's memorial. When she accidentally knocked off his favorite fishing cap, he was almost bald. His constant hat had left a tan line.

"I'm so glad you're here. I was going to look you up once I got settled." She kissed his stubbly weathered cheek.

"Oh sure, that's what all the ladies say. Not one has called since your Aunt Hattie...left." Grief filled his reddened, sagging eyes.

"I know we all miss her." She patted his shoulder.

"More than ya'll ever know. When she started losing it mentally, that was harder to watch than if she'd been struck by a damn heart attack. I pray to God some whale eats me when it's my time and not put me in one of those homes for old folks. Not me."

"None of us want to watch our loved ones go through that. So, tell me. How have you been?"

"Ornery as ever. Doing the same thing I've done for the last seventy years. Filling and pulling traps, catching a few stripers and bluefish. Selling to my best customer,

The Lobster Pound down on Manomet Point. Love working with those folks.

"Dead of winter I sat down at Brewers and listened to tall fish tales while those young mechanics threw a fit at the engines they had to repair. Drooled over the boats they were getting ready for the boat shows in Boston and Providence." He snickered. "These stiff ole' fingers made it tough to work on my handmade tube, worm, and Christmas tree rigs."

He'd made a wonderful Santa Claus with shoulder length silver hair and wiry beard, especially if he'd been out catching chub for live wells for ice fishing.

"I'd like to be a fly on the wall to hear what you guys talk about all day." She winked and rolled her eyes.

"So, pumpkin, I can only guess what brought ya to town. Sure miss your Aunt Hattie. One of the finest women I've ever met, even though she could be a cantankerous old bat some days."

"I know. What great friends you were all those years. I think she'd gone to the nursing home years before if you hadn't been here to help."

A fleck of moisture fell from his right droopy eye. "Yep, one fine woman. The good Lord broke the mold when he made her. Ya sure remind me of her. I remember those summers ya'd come and stay, highlight of her year."

"So blessed to have had her in my life for as long as I did." She gazed around the room. "So, what in the hell am I going to do, Captain Maz? She left me her most valued treasure. I barely have enough money to get a bag of groceries right now. I'm fighting my own financial woes.

"Then on top of everything, some damn corporation claimed they bought the house for back taxes and it doesn't belong to me. Things have gone from bad to worse since the day I got here. Not to mention someone struck me over the head."

"Jus' hold on now. Let's take one calamity at a time. What's about ya getting hit over the head?"

"First night back in town I stopped at the house. Someone struck me on the head and knocked me out."

"Jesus-geez. Were ya hurt badly? Why'd someone want to do that?"

"Your guess is as good as mine. The police so far have brushed it under the rug and kept it pretty quiet from what I can tell. They're saying maybe some plaster fell from the ceiling and hit me since it was pretty windy out. Must've become disoriented and crawled to the street. I don't remember a damn thing."

"I'll be checking up on that. I've heard 'bout that company buying land on the upper East Coast building monstrosity condos, destroying precious land and memories. There's obviously a big mistake. I witnessed Hattie's will. She left ya this house outright."

"I know. My attorney said it was a done deal, but then this Rod Kesson guy shows up and tells me differently. Anyway, I'm letting the legal guys do their thing. I've started cleaning the debris left by the tenants, shame on them. I think there are raccoons under the Mansard roof. Heard noises up there."

He squeezed her shoulder. "Your Aunt Hattie would be proud. She always was. You've got the same fire in ya gut she had. Yeah, the renters need to be hung by the rafters for leaving this place in such a mess. Can't trust anyone these days. Heard they tapped the neighbor's electric and kept a bunch of dogs for pay."

"I'm doing my best, but to be honest, I don't know how to even begin this whole process of restoration. First, I don't have the financial resources nor the know how to try to get any government aid or have it listed as a historical house. Get it on the national registry maybe.

"Heaven help me. I don't know if I have the stamina. I'm totally overwhelmed right now. Your broad shoulder came along at the perfect time." She placed a peck on his rugged cheek and embraced him.

"Darlin', I understand where ya're coming from. But, I'm going to tell ya a secret. And it's just between us."

"Yeah?"

"You can't breathe one word of this. Hattie and I kept it between us and no one must find out."

"You've got my attention. So, what's the secret?"

CHAPTER 12

Rod slipped out of his black Mercedes onto the pebbly driveway of the mansion. He'd considered driving the Denali, but it was a perfect day for the convertible.

Kelli's corroded Jeep was parked in the overgrown weeds at the back of the house. This wasn't easy to eat crow, but when it came to projects and his father's contentment, he had a job to do. He couldn't let personal feelings interfere, even though he empathized with her situation.

Is that why I find her so attractive? I feel sorry for her?

He rapped on the open wooden door. "Hello?"

"Come in," echoed from the two-story foyer.

Perched at the top of the staircase, which overlooked the foyer, Kelli had broom in hand and was bent at the waist which exposed trim legs. When she swept the debris, dust flew around in circles.

How apropos? She carries a broom.

He couldn't distinguish if her disheveled strands were meant to be hip or whether it was a bad hair day. Her shoulder length copper-colored hair appeared natural curly, but he never guessed what was natural, surgically or chemically enhanced on a woman anymore. He'd bet money she feasted on cranberries from local bogs, raised her own chickens, and gathered nuts.

"Kelli, sorry to intrude, but may I have a moment of your time?"

"Well, if it isn't Rod Kesson." She gloated while she strolled down the stairway. "Please come in."

Even though a hard woman to figure out, she was easy on the eyes. Summer highlights emphasized high cheekbones and large, baby-blue eyes. He wasn't sure of her heritage, but her skin had a bronze glow with few age spots which indicated she probably hadn't spent much time in the sun.

"I apologize for stopping by unannounced, but I had no way to reach you. Hope it's not a bad time."

"You stopping by at a bad time? Always."

He admired her spunkiness and willingness to speak her mind. She didn't appear intimidated.

"I bet you came to apologize about the screw up your big shot attorneys made who claimed you owned my property."

"Actually, yes, I came to explain how all that transpired, but came on another matter too."

"And what other matter would we have to discuss?"

"A lucrative financial one for you."

"Lucrative, huh? I doubt it."

"Is there someplace where we can sit and talk? Perhaps over dinner?"

"I don't usually eat dinner. I've got a couple of lawn chairs out front."

"Whatever floats your boat," he joked.

He followed her out the front door, down the creaky steps, and onto the lawn where two unsteady mesh chairs were propped under an old tree.

"Sure it's safe to sit under? Looks like the bark has fallen off and the limbs don't look too sturdy either?"

"As a matter of fact, this tree is over a century old. It's an El Gingko. You don't see many of them around anymore."

A slight breeze caused loose chestnut pods to tumble from the tree when he glanced up. From his viewpoint, it appeared it needed to be whacked down, not preserved.

"May I get you a bottled water?"

"Thanks, I'm fine. I want you to know the error wasn't my legal team. Apparently, the title company had a new employee who didn't do their due diligence. That's when they take reasonable steps to satisfy legal requirements."

"Thank you, but I'm college educated." She raised her eyebrows. "I know what due diligence is."

"Well, an error was made. I could go into greater detail, but the bottom line is I apologize. I'll have a letter from my legal counsel in a few hours that'll give an explanation what transpired."

"Apology accepted." She shifted in the uneven chair.

"I'm here to offer you an extravagant amount to sell this land and house to my company. We originally purchased for back taxes which amounted to over ten grand. Given the circumstances and situation you're facing, my company is willing to write you a check for four million, giving us immediate and full ownership of the acreage and mansion, which will be demolished."

She dropped her bottled water. "Excuse me?"

"We're offering you four million for the land and house. It would cost you easily half that much to restore and maintain. I understand that money would give you financial security for the rest of your life."

"What do you mean you understand?"

"It's my business to check out potential sellers. I know you've had tough losses over the last five years. This would give you not only financial stability, but assure your son and his family the same."

"Stability, security? My son and his family?" She stood up. Her fiery eyes locked with his. "What in the hell do you know about my stability and family, Mr. Kesson?

There is *no* amount of money that will make me give up this land. Nada. So, you can take your offer, jump back in that piece of foreign metal, and drive your merry little ass back to wherever."

He was dumb stricken. How often would a lady in grievous circumstances coldly turn down four million for a piece of land and house beyond repair? And have the balls to call him out?

She was even more attractive when mad. She crossed her arms across her chest. He suppressed his laughter, but admired her gutsiness. If his father had been here to see her in action, he might have been swayed.

"This offer is only good for a week. Perhaps you should not make a hasty decision. Discuss it with your son, financial representative, attorney. Here's my card. You can reach me at any time if you want to discuss. I hope for you and your family's sake you won't pass up this opportunity for financial security. You'd be making a huge mistake."

"If I make a mistake, it's my responsibility, not yours. Thanks for the offer, but no thanks. Have a great day."

He stood up, stuck out his hand, which she ignored. He mumbled all the way back to the car. His father was going to be infuriated. He was sure to get an earful. It would give his father another opportunity to reprimand him for not being able to get the job done.

The girl though, that could be another matter entirely.

CHAPTER 13

Kelli trembled while the Mercedes drove out of sight. This was her land and now her home, regardless of its condition. She was mad at herself for allowing him into her thoughts. He made her second guess herself.

But, she had to face reality. Sure, legally it was hers, but along with that came responsibility for renovation and restoration of the deteriorated mansion. How in the world could she accomplish that or keep up with property taxes?

She giggled at her valiant exchange with Rod Kesson. Was she a friggin' idiot? If her family knew she'd been offered four mil and turned it down on the spot, they'd want to put her away. Would they be upset knowing she threw away financial security for them? Her gut wrenched. Why did this man have this effect on her? Did she let pride and her emotional state influence her decision?

No. She'd make this work. She had to. Not only for Auntie, but to prove to herself she was strong and could survive through worse case scenarios. And more importantly, for her self-esteem and preservation.

She contemplated what she'd do with that kind of money. First on her list would be a new home for her son and his family. Second, every child in her extended family would be ensured a college education. Third, she'd be extremely charitable with organizations that needed help, especially those involved with children or cancer.

If she splurged for herself, it'd be awesome to purchase a five bedroom, five bath home with a screened in pool on Florida's gulf coast on the beach. For once she'd be able to house her son and his family with space to spare or anyone else who wanted to visit. Plus, she'd have unlimited funds to entertain. Yes, that would be amazing.

As a second home...Lake Tahoe would be perfect. She'd buy a log cabin in the mountains that overlooked the lake. It'd have an imposing stone fireplace to burn wood where she'd enjoy the aroma and allow tranquil time when needed. She fantasized she'd probably need to keep a condo and small home in Indiana and Illinois to be close to family and her long-time friends. The list would go on.

But she *was* dreaming. She couldn't break her promise to Auntie. That was worth more than any amount of money, wasn't it? Had she made a terrible mistake? Should she reconsider? She had a week.

She had one more box to sift through before dinner. A turkey sandwich with mayonnaise was in the cooler she'd bought since the kitchen had been gutted after a fire a few years ago. Barbeque chips and diet Coke completed her meal. She spread the paper towel on an antique steamer dotted with old stickers from overseas travel and placed her dinner on it. Inside the trunk were old books she couldn't wait to look through to see who the authors were and what they were about.

She sat on the long, Victorian fainting couch she was surprised the tenants left. They obviously had no idea of its value with hand-crafted wood trimmed on top and gold brocade fabric. It was in surprisingly good condition.

The tenants had sloppily boxed up and stacked most of Auntie's possessions in a small room on the third floor which faced the street. It'd probably take her years to go through it all. If Auntie had a fault, she never got rid of anything and might be considered a hoarder nowadays. At least, she'd been clean, even though dusty and disorganized. The homestead didn't have the same welcoming feeling as when Auntie was alive. Kelli was overwhelmed with melancholy.

The sun was setting. Flashes of orange, honey, and rose reflected through the soiled windows onto the peeling wallpaper, lending the impression the house was ablaze.

The north and east front parlors downstairs contained double French doors that led to the wrap-around veranda which was now missing the floor on the north side due to water, harsh winters in Massachusetts, and termites. A cool light wind filtered through. She forced the warped doors so she could lock them. No wonder the house was easy prey unoccupied.

A familiar fragrance wafted through the room which surprised her. It was similar to Auntie's favorite perfume, Pilkeke, which she purchased in Hawaii in her early twenties. The scent was a combination of exotic sweet tropical flowers. Dust balls swirled on the wooden floor. Pieces of trash rose in the air, creating a mini wind tornado.

Something brushed against her back. What was that? Had her imagination got the best of her? She spun around. Nothing was there.

Was that a giggle and bell ringing? Did it come from the staircase? Goosebumps grazed her spine. When she turned to grab her sandwich, the wrapper was there. The sandwich, barbecue chips, and Coke had disappeared.

~ ~ ~

Sleeping in the mansion for the first night was unnerving. She couldn't afford to stay at the Blue Spruce indefinitely, even though the owners had been exceptionally gracious and reduced the cost of the room. Everyone in this small community was fond of Hattie and the mansion. That was one thing she loved about this village—everyone came together when someone was in need.

The northeast corner second floor room was turned into her temporary bedroom. Even though a beautiful antique four poster bed and worn mattress occupied the room, she purchased a blow-up, sleeping bag, top sheet, and pillow.

Being a germ-a-phobe, it wasn't an option to sleep on a mattress other people or critters had used. The mattress would be the first thing thrown out of the house, if they ever delivered the oversized metal dumpster. She hauled supplies and boxes up and down the tall staircase which was labor intensive, but gave a sense of accomplishment. She was grateful for the cool breeze.

The bedroom's windows were in dire shape along with the others. The lofty arched front window that faced the street had one of four panes boarded up. How sad the other window, which had been a stained glass showcase at one time, was now covered with plywood. Twice the size of the front window, small pieces of stained glass had been designed to depict the sea and sun. Soft-hued colors reflected prisms throughout the room on a bright day. As a child, it reminded her of attending church on a sunny morning; each frame glowed with colors alluding to a message from God.

It was nine before she realized, but it hadn't been that long since the sun set. Thankfully, summer days were extended this time of year. She latched the front doors. There was no need to worry about the back and side doors since they were boarded up to keep out animals and kids who looked for a place to party.

It had cooled considerably from the high of seventy-five. A brisk northeast breeze glided through the sliding screen Auntie used in the bottom of the windows to keep out bugs. She was fortunate to pry the fragile window open without busting the frame or glass.

Damn the electric company. They said it'd only be a few days before service was turned on. They gave her hogwash about not up to code, fire hazard, blah, blah, blah. All she wanted was to be able to see and maneuver in the dark.

The hardware store on State Road had the supplies she needed. She hated to spend the money, but was grateful to have a heavy-duty flashlight right now. The house was dreadfully dark, set back at least one-hundred-fifty yards from the road, no lights on or near the property.

She bounced when she sat on the blow-up bed. Remnants of bug spray lingered which caused her eyes to water and sinuses ache, similar to her chronic sinus infections. She didn't care. It was one thing to sleep in the house alone for the first time, but to think bugs might crawl on her was beyond her tolerance level.

After she wiped her feet with a disinfectant towel, one of her quirky habits before bedtime, she slipped off her grimy dungaree shorts and blouse and replaced them with an oversized tee shirt. She was tired but mentally more relaxed.

The sheet was cool to her feet and welcomed her fatigued body. She flipped off the flashlight and laid there, staring at a ceiling black as ink.

Preternatural sounds reverberated throughout the house. Her greatest fear was raccoons or other critters had taken up space in the Mansard roof. She hadn't been this scared since she'd slept in a tent for the first time at a Girl Scout retreat at ten. Maybe it was spirits?

She had deep rooted beliefs the universe was so colossal there had to be life on other planets, so it stood to reason there could be life on other invisible planes. It was entirely plausible spirits existed, who moved at will through time from place to place. Given all the junctures to choose from, it was a small wonder she'd met one. She'd never shared with anyone, other than Hattie, she believed she'd seen Belinda from time to time when she visited Auntie in the summers.

She soothed her mind and visualized her son, his wife, and grandchildren, the loves of her life. Last time they were together, they had spent an entire weekend frolicking at the pool at her small nine-hole country club. Now a widow, it was one of the few places she was comfortable by herself since she'd known most of the members for years. The granddaughters reminded her so much of her son, true water lovers, unhappy when it was time to go home. While separated by miles, she chatted with them almost daily and often used Facetime.

Steve and she had waited almost four years after marriage to have a family in order to provide a stable environment. Their son was the greatest gift and she couldn't imagine life without him. When he married and had two beautiful children, her circle of life was complete. They brought immense joy.

As any mother would, she wanted to protect her son from the hurts of the world. She had no intention of telling him what his father had done. What purpose would that serve other than destroy precious memories he needed to last a lifetime?

She couldn't have asked for a better father to her son. Even though Steve worked long hours and required him to be out of town, the family time they spent together was quality, if not quantity.

An avid outdoorsman, he enjoyed boating, fishing, and camping. Those were family activities and now their son passed on those to his girls.

Steve was raised by loving Catholic parents and was the third in a family of ten. His parents instilled extraordinary values—honesty, integrity, others before self. She was proud of the man Steve had become—until his accident. Maybe that was why it was so hard to believe what he'd done. She still remained close to her in-laws and participated in family celebrations and holidays. Perhaps her immediate family was the driving force to pursue the mansion's renovations. Maybe Hattie was right after all.

Her body relaxed as she meditated and practiced breathing techniques; the eerie sounds drifted away. Grainy eyes shut, she pulled the sheet close to her chin even though it was still warm outside.

The dream was so real. The moment was etched in her memory, the setting like an old movie. Auntie had taken her on the front porch a week after her sixteenth birthday. It was hot, no wind for relief which caused her shorts and shirt to stick to her skinny body.

Darkness fell and fireflies flitted around the yard and porch. Prisms from the oil lamp flashed on the covered porch dotted with overflowing pots of impatiens, geraniums, and ferns. The pink lemonade was warm. The ice had melted quickly. Auntie was alive, maybe mid-fifties.

"Comfy, sweetheart?" her auntie asked.

She tucked the throw around her legs and curled in the white wicker chair. A chilly breeze swirled around her. "Yep, snug as a bug in a rug," she teased, one of her aunt's favorite sayings.

Her aunt's laugh was one of a kind. Deep and addicting, it came from her soul.

"So, tell me the story of Belinda and Joshua," she asked for the umpteenth time.

"This story is between us. No repeating to anyone, you hear me? Well, once upon a time...there was a young lady, Belinda. Her father was a wealthy and powerful man having inherited money from generations and invested wisely in ships, railroads, stocks, and banks in the mid 1800's.

"Tough old bird, of the old school. No one dared to cross him. He used his wealth to buy local politicians to advance his financial and political gains. He wasn't admired or liked by many. In fact, most people were afraid of him.

"Records indicate he purchased the land the mansion sits on. Back then when someone bought up that much acreage and splurged on a house of this magnitude, it was unheard of.

"Shortly after the mansion was built, and believe me in that day it was truly a mansion, they had their first child, a son named Kent. That's all a man ever wanted, a son to carry on the family legacy and business. Kent was killed in a freak hunting accident at fifteen here on the estate. Rumors had it Captain Eldridge never was right after that.

"No parent should ever have to bury a child, that's for sure. They said Kent's grave is on the estate, but no one knows where now. There was a small fence around the cemetery at one time, but the tombstone's lost. It must've been grown over.

"Belinda was two years younger than her brother, and of course, being a girl she was Captain Eldridge's little princess. From the rumors handed down generations, after his son was killed Captain Eldridge became obsessed with the safety of Belinda and constantly had her supervised.

"Guess she was quite the tomboy and adventurer. Loved to play hide-and-seek in the trees and bushes. Scuttlebutt was once while hiding from her brother, it got dark and she got lost. They naturally assumed she'd been kidnapped for ransom. Captain Eldridge became deranged.

"Well, to make a long story short, Belinda met a young man, Joshua Jones. Joshua was from the wrong side of the tracks, not an aristocrat like Captain Eldridge who planned to marry his daughter to a local man's son, so she'd be married into the family of his choosing with wealth and social status.

"That didn't fly with Belinda, a born rebel. She fell in love with Joshua and snuck around. While her mother didn't want to go against her husband's wishes, she turned a blind eye, knowing Belinda was seeing Joshua."

She was enthralled with the love story, especially with Auntie's excitement via her voice. It was like Hattie had lived in this era.

"You know the rest of the story. Belinda conceived out of wedlock, taboo those days in Eldridge's social circles. When Captain Eldridge found out, he arranged Joshua's demise. The story was Joshua had gone on a whaling expedition and was killed at sea when a rogue hit the boat. Washed him overboard where he drowned. His body was never recovered, likely consumed by companion orca that frequented the waters.

"When Belinda was told Joshua died at sea, she was devastated and didn't believe her father, who knew she was pregnant and forbid her to keep the child. Back in the day it was a family disgrace to have an unwed daughter with child. Her father planned to force her into a home for unwed mothers, have the child, and give it up for adoption.

"According to folklore, and the story has been handed down so long who knows the real truth, there was a confrontation between Belinda and Captain Eldridge. He claimed she accidentally fell off the bluff over there." Her aunt nodded toward the bay.

"So the tale goes for a century and a half, Belinda walked the widow's walk on full moons yearning for Joshua to return."

Kelli was roused from the lifelike dream by a voice whispering, "You're in danger."

She couldn't move. Was this her imagination? Was she still dreaming? If she didn't move, maybe she'd wake up. She kept her eyes closed.

"Joshua's coming back. They can't destroy my home. He has to be able to find me," the voice explained.

She focused on the voice. It wasn't her imagination; it was real. She slowly rolled to her side. With the three-paned window behind her back, the full moon illuminated the room and cast a bright silhouette. A transparently thin young woman in a long red dress emerged; the moonbeam resonated through her.

Stricken with terror, Kelli was afraid to move as sweat dripped off her brow. Her throat constricted. Vomit rose in her throat. Was she having a total meltdown? Why was she so scared? Was this the same mist she'd seen as a child? Her eyes watered; she couldn't see. She wanted to speak, but couldn't. Fear encapsulated her.

And then as quickly as the vision had come it disappeared.

Afraid to sleep, she tossed and turned until the next morning. Her body was stiff with dull pains in her legs from the tension. Her head pulsed, similar to when she was in her twenties and had gone to an all-night party with alcohol and no sleep. Wrapped tightly in her blanket, she was so hot her tee shirt clung from sweat.

What happened last night? Was I so fatigued I thought I saw Belinda? And the dream with Auntie—it was so real. Am I delusional?

CHAPTER 14

How in the hell was he going to explain his failure to close the deal to his father? After all, it wasn't his fault since his father had chosen the counsel on this project.

Rod's personal Lear jet landed on the tarmac of the private airport in Hilton Head, South Carolina. The routine was for the white limo to wait for his arrival. He clutched his black leather briefcase and exited down the metal stairs. It was a typical beach day, light sea breeze, high humidity, and sunshine aplenty. Now, if his father's disposition was half as bright, he might be home free.

One of his parents' five homes, located throughout the world, was in a gated community next to the Atlantic Ocean and consisted of five acres. No neighbors were close except the private golf course located to the north which exposed the island signature hole par three.

He checked his Galaxy Note for messages while they pulled into the circular drive. He hoped Kelli Goddard had left a voice mail denoting she'd changed her mind and accepted his offer. If that were the case, he'd be seen the hero, not a disappointment through his father's eyes. There was no message.

"We're here, Mr. Kesson," the limo driver announced.

He inhaled deeply to lessen the anxiety built up on the hour and half flight, even though he consumed two vodka martinis. He didn't look forward to what was in store from his father. The forever blabber of his inability to close business deals, mistakes he'd made along the process, and, of course, the disappointment his father would vent on this project—and the past.

"Hi, sweetheart," his mother squealed.

It was like Christmas every time she saw him; she wasn't shy to show affection to her only child. She trotted quickly towards him when he entered the two-story marble foyer. The stately staircase was the focal point, stairs up each side accented with spindles of twisted wrought iron. A one-of-a-kind walnut handcrafted round table sat in the middle with fresh yellow and white roses and baby's breath.

"Hi, Mom. How are you?"

"Jus' wonderful now that ya'll are home. I still miss ya every time ya're away from ya mama," she teased and winked.

"Oh, Mom. You make me blush." He picked up her tiny frame and kissed her wrinkled cheek.

"And do I hear a familiar voice in here?" echoed from the two-story family room.

"Ya father has been waitin' for ya to get here. What kind of big deal are ya two brewing up now?"

Here we go. Again. He exhaled.

"Hi, Son." His father extended his large hand and squeezed tightly.

"Hi, Dad." Never a hug, just the decorum of etiquette, even though related.

"Come on in. Let's sit outside and get some of this great southern air and watch those jerks that take my money every week come up hole four. If they ever dive for balls around that island green, they'd make a fortune and stop these hefty damn assessments."

He grinned at his dad's attempted joke, but it was only a prelude to the upcoming dreaded business discussion.

"Mickey, can you get us two Dewars on the rocks, please," the elder Kesson instructed the appropriately attired butler. His dad tapped him on the back before they sat in expensive brown wicker chairs dotted with cushions in coastal beach colors.

The two-story wrap-around porch contained an elevated fire pit and overlooked a sunken swimming pool. The concrete dolphin spouted water, an impressive backdrop to the white sand and ocean in the distance.

He'd had many parties at this house growing up when his parents were out of town, which was often. Thank God, Bessie, the housekeeper, loved him like her own and covered for him. Out of their homes, except the one in the Bahamas, this was his favorite since this was where he graduated. He'd attended a private school in Hilton Head supported solely by wealthy parents. His mother had been convinced he had attention deficit disorder since he had trouble focusing and sitting still. He spent many an hour after school with tutors.

Football had been his favorite sport and he played quarterback his junior and senior years. He spent more time with trainers than on the field. His father prepped him for success and college.

"So, let's get down to business, young man. What's the latest on the project in Manomet? Everything squared away?"

He swallowed hard. "So, you haven't talked to Troy?"

"No, Son. I left this in your hands to get this unfortunate complication resolved."

He almost choked on the large swig of his drink and sat down the crystal glass harder than expected on the tiled circular table. "Well, Dad, we've got a problem—"

"I don't want to hear 'bout problems, Son. I want to hear 'bout results."

"Sometimes you have to work through the problem to get results, and that's what I'm faced with right now.

Legally, she owns the house. Hattie Hubbard willed the property to Kelli Goddard, but no new deed was written or recorded at the Plymouth County Registry conveying the property, so Kelli owns by default virtue.

"When BKC scanned the registries up and down the coast, we jumped on taking a prime piece, according to the assessor's records for tax redemption. The collector could've cared less who paid the back taxes. Unfortunately, our quick action this time didn't work out to our advantage. She's the owner. So, to make a long story short, I offered her four mil for the property. She flat out declined the offer."

His father jumped out of the chair. "So, who gives a damn if she legally owns the property and house. There's no way anyone would turn down an offer of four mil, especially for that shit-ass wreck. She'd have to be a pretty stupid broad." His deep voice elevated while he paced in his expensive loafers on the tiled slate.

"This lady isn't stupid. She has principles and roots in this property and house. There's a lot more to the story, but she's not willing to sell and that's all there is to it. I gave her a week to reconsider. Suggested she obtain professional help to evaluate this offer."

"Damn, Rodney," his father shouted. "Haven't you learned by now everyone has a price? I'll bet you a thousand dollars if I met with that lady, I'd have her eatin' out of my hand and the sale consummated within half a day."

"Well, if you think I'm so incompetent, then perhaps you should try just that." He scooted back the chair and stood up. "As a matter of fact, I think that's an excellent idea. Mickey, can you serve me a double in the house, please?"

"Rodney Kesson, don't walk out on this conversation," his father hollered.

Some things would never change.

"Dad, it doesn't make any difference what I come up with or what I want to do to resolve a problem, you cut me off at the knees. You micro manage. I've got a plan that might work, but no…let's scold Rodney and alienate him. Let someone else pick up the pieces. Is that your plan, Dad?"

"Well, no. We need this problem resolved like yesterday. Two hundred million is wrapped up with investors on this condominium and marina project. Investors are climbing up my back wanting dates they can expect to be in. I can't keep telling them my son is working on it, now can I?"

"You're the Chairman of the Board. You can tell them whatever the hell you want. Tell them we've hit a snag. You'll come up with something."

"I give you one week and you better have the paperwork to that property. We can go up to five million if we have to, but that's the top limit."

"One week. Five million. It'll be a done deal." He strolled into the house, shook his head and wiped the sweat off his brow.

His father would eventually be the death of him, if not sooner.

CHAPTER 15

Even after fifty plus years, Sam Mazalewski never complained about getting up at three-thirty a.m. The early sea worm got the bass, he always said.

Following his daily routine, he drove to the bait truck on the wharf and prepped for the day by loading totes on his boat with his stern man, Tim. Though dark, they motored to his mooring in the skiff to reach his lobster boat, the *TNT*. While they steamed to the fishing grounds and his trawls, fluorescent phosphorus illuminated his wake and left light which acknowledged his passage. He loved every second.

Rough weather wasn't the issue at his age. It was the cold that affected his rheumatoid arthritis. When it coursed throughout his body, it caused his joints to tighten and his knees to swell. For an old fart, he was lucky he didn't take many drugs to keep the old ticker going, but recently he was forced to see a doctor for RA pain. Between the stiffness and pain in his joints, especially his hands and feet, he took a prescription which he cursed at daily.

Ten traps in a contiguous haul, they gaffed buoy after buoy and pulled each trap onboard to check for bait. When he was young and in his prime physically, he had close to eight hundred traps under his commercial license. He was lucky if he had half that now, which was demanding for his age and physical ailments. But what else would he do? Nothing. He hated daytime TV.

He could perform the routine with his eyes closed. Pull up a trap, measure and band the lobster, discard ones too short or eggers, and re-bait the trap. Once each trap was prepped, off the stern they went, buoys dropped from either end. Keeper lobsters were thrown in oxygenated live wells where ocean water recirculated and kept them alive since sometimes they were on the water for over ten hours or more. Once at the wharf, they tied up, threw their catch in totes, and hauled them up to be weighed.

"Well, how ya doing there, Bud?" he asked the young man from The Lobster Pound.

"Fine, Captain. Did you have a good day?" He weighed the totes and wrote out their slip of pounds for the day's catch.

"You tell me," he teased when handed the paper. "Appears you'll get a pretty good check at the end of the week if you keep this up."

"Sure hope so. Gotta make it while able."

"I'll second that," Tim yelled while he hosed down the boat of bait juice and debris. "My wife is about to go into labor, so I'll be out of commission for a while. Better crack it while we can." His helper inventoried what they needed for the next day.

"Yepper. Those diesel engine repairs last week sure cut into my profits," Sam complained. Consumers had no idea the overhead and aggravation this romance with the sea cost.

They shuttled to the mooring, got into the skiff, returned to the dinghy dock, and tied up for the night. He limped home that evening after more than eight hours on the water which was rougher than usual. He wasn't sure if his overall illness was the arthritis or the new medication, but he was grumpy.

Or was it there was no one to go back to? Hattie often had him over with fine meals on the table and always welcomed him with open arms. God, what a good woman. He sure did miss her.

~ ~ ~

Sam was in a great deal of pain the following day, so Tim and his brother-in-law made the rounds. Extra bucks were welcomed with a new baby on the way.

He loved breakfast at Marshlands at the intersection of Old Beach Road and State Road. He'd been going there for coffee and breakfast forever, other than when Hattie fed him at the mansion, more often than not. She spoiled him with his favorites—homemade French toast with fresh blueberries, honey cured bacon or sausage, Chock Full of Nuts coffee, and freshly squeezed orange juice.

He liked it best when she leaned over in the younger years. Nostalgia overwhelmed him when he thought of her, such a sweet soul. He regretted not making her his wife, but Hattie would have none of that, being independent and stubborn as the day was long. Maybe that was why they got along so well for over seventy years. They were the last living natives who were born and resided their entire lives in Manomet. People nowadays moved often, similar to birds migrating south. Plus, they shared a passion of the land and sea, the last, something most people never truly connected with.

One of his fondest memories was their annual trek to P'town to watch the carnival parade. It'd become a tradition with their friends. The group met in Plymouth at the dock where the Harbor Master's shack was located.

He'd empty his lobster boat of bait, traps, warps, culling tables or anything with an odor which allowed ample space for twenty guests, their chairs and coolers.

The last trip had been on a beautiful morning, perfect for a boat ride. The seas were calm. The thirty-two foot boat's bow protected the riders who sat in lawn chairs in the stern. Some hung out on top of the cabin.

Being out on the seas was one of their favorite past times, even though he spent many hours working the lobster pots. Hattie loved when they trolled, so she could see the old lighthouses. One in particular, tagged the Bug Light, was used by the Coast Guard which aided ships over the years to avoid rocks and cliffs.

The trip took about ninety minutes and allowed their friends time to chat and eat while the youngsters consumed road sodas. When they reached the harbor, he'd moor the boat and a launch brought the occupants to shore, having to make two trips.

The docks were crammed with revelers toting chairs and umbrellas in case of a summer thunderstorm. They made their way to Main Street, which was packed, and were fortunate to set up chairs in front of the courthouse.

The group usually broke into smaller clans. Some went to local bars and restaurants to pass the time until the parade. Others wandered, shopped, and took pictures of participants in costumes which reflected this year's theme, Las Vegas. For hours partakers mingled in costumes which ranged from Elvis to Siegfried and Roy, some painted to resemble white lions in their act. Floats tossed colored beads which struck giddy onlookers.

The ride home was by far more interesting. Dusk arrived with a north wind which whipped breakers against the white hull, spraying passengers, chilling those that had not brought yellow slickers or Grundens. Phosphorous glowed in the wake after dark which created neo-green specks of fluorescent.

"And what are you day dreaming about, Captain?" Kelli asked.

Startled, he turned to find Hattie's niece next to him. Her warm hand glided across his shoulder which ached, then squeezed, causing him to cough. He welcomed the feminine touch.

"Oh, just pullin' out some ole' memories of Hattie and the good times we had," he explained.

Kelli slid across from him in the booth that'd been beaten and scratched over the eighty years the restaurant had been open. Everyone in that small village had carved their initials in the wood, some with hearts. It was one of several booths they kept from the original restaurant.

Because the food was supreme, they added on to the building to accommodate their expanding clientele, especially during tourist season. Even though Auntie's pies were to die for, theirs surpassed hers.

A wrought iron holder contained salt, pepper, artificial sweeteners, hot sauce, and paper towels and waited for the next patron to slather on ingredients. Homemade valances of orange and brown hues covered partially fogged windows which steamed from the home cooking.

"Some lady, that woman. Had the best heart and soul of anyone I've ever known. But if you crossed her, she had a tongue that'd cut you down and never look back. Damn I miss her. Should've been me to go first, not her."

Kelli stretched out her arm and grabbed his hand. Her fingers were smooth like a baby's butt compared to his weathered and callused fingers. She caressed his tendons, followed deep crevices. She must've inherited that special touch from Hattie, even though Hattie's hands were damaged from years of hard physical labor, pulling lobster pots in the sun and tending her land.

"Oh, Captain, stop that nonsense. We don't get to make those choices in life. I miss Auntie too, but there's not a damn thing we can do about it, other than honor her wishes. I don't know how in the hell I'm going to do that."

"I betcha you're resourceful like Hattie was." He smiled playfully. "I mean she'd cook up a meal with barely anything in that big old house. Something else, that woman."

"That she was."

A teenager approached the table with a pad and grabbed a pen out of the pocket of her apron. "Okay, Captain Maz, I can only guess you're having the same thing you had yesterday and the day before?"

"Sweetie, ya sure know how to make an old fella feel special."

"Since you practically come in every morning, it's not a difficult order to remember," she teased. "Ma'am, what would you like?"

"Why don't you call me, Kelli. I'll take a short stack of blueberry pancakes, two pieces of sausage, black coffee, small orange juice too, please."

"Leaded or decaf?"

"Leaded and cream."

"Have your coffee right out," the girl cheerfully responded.

He glanced at Kelli, her eyes puffy and red. Stress permeated her dainty face.

"Sweetheart, you okay? You're looking jus' a bit pale today. Sorry we didn't get to finish our conversation the other day since we were interrupted by that meter reader from the power company. Hope they get your power up and running soon."

She tinkered with the knife and fork and wiggled nervously. "Yeah, me too. You've certainly piqued my curiosity. I don't know, Captain. I'm overwhelmed with everything that's happened since I got here. It's like a bad omen. Maybe I shouldn't try to restore the mansion. Perhaps I should take the offer and get the hell out of Dodge while I still have my sanity."

"Offer?"

"Rod Kesson offered me four million for the land and house, but don't repeat that, please."

"Four million dollars? Holy Moly," he exclaimed. "And...what was your answer?"

"You know me better than that. Of course, it was no. But, how in the world can I come up with that kind of money to restore the house? Four million and I could walk away a financially secure woman. I haven't been that since my husband died."

His heart bled for her. The agony in her voice and facial expressions confirmed she still grieved for the husband tragically lost prematurely. He'd heard through the grapevine circumstances of his death and her financial tribulations.

He grasped her hand. "Kelli, yar're like a daughter to me. Always have been and always will. Is there anything I can do to help? I've got a few bucks left."

She locked widened eyes with him. A smile emerged across her face. "Well, if you buy a lottery ticket and win, can I take out a loan?" she joked.

"Honey, if I win the lottery, yar'll be the first to know and no loan needed." He squeezed her hand.

The young waitress returned with two white mugs of steaming coffee and a bowl of plastic containers filled with cream.

"Thanks, Becky."

"You're welcome, Captain."

"I don't know where to turn, where to go with all of this. Auntie mentioned she started the process of investigating federal and state grants to see if she might qualify for funds to aid in the cost of restoration."

"Yeah, I remember her talking 'bout that. If I recall correctly, she gave Carolyn Ball around one-hundred-fifty bucks to get online and search companies for grants. Ya know how Hattie avoided computers like the plague," he joked.

"That she did."

"I was there one afternoon when Carolyn stopped over. She'd spent an entire weekend culling historical, housing, and open space opportunities from the list. She told Hattie she'd have to fill out reams of applications and provide supporting documentation. I'd guess that's when Hattie dropped the ball."

"Well, guess I can try to get a hold of Carolyn and see what she can tell me since I can't ask…Auntie." Sadness filled her voice.

"I know, sweetie." He patted her on the back. "We all miss her."

"Better get busy and get the trash out of the house. Can't believe the renters almost stripped her clean of furnishings and left one hell of a mess. The Wilsons stopped by and offered to help. They felt bad they hadn't checked up more on the house since Hattie went into the nursing home, but they're usually only here in the summers. Guess he had health issues too over the last few years."

"Honey, let me see what I can find out. I know there are a lot of locals that'd be thrilled to see that goddess restored. I'm a bettin' we can get ya some help. It's a damn shame it got in that state to begin with. Hattie'd be rollin' in her grave, if she had one. Still gives me shivers she donated her body to science and where she might be, but that was her choice."

"I have to tell you, I had an interesting conversation with the Blythes next door. I'm sure you know them."

"Sure, Brian and Beth. Kind of strange, but friendly enough. Stay to themselves, but showed up every now and then over at Hattie's in the summer. What about 'em?"

"Beth came over while I took a break outside yesterday. She said for me to watch out. The house was haunted. Do you believe that?"

He shifted on the hard wooden bench; his bad knees ached from sitting too long. His arthritic back tensed. "Haunted, hmm?"

"That's what she said. Belinda Eldridge paces the widow's walk on nights with a full moon."

"Is that so? What do ya—"

Gregg strutted into the restaurant and headed directly to their booth, interrupting his chain of thought.

"Well, hello there, Gregg. Imagine meeting ya here," he joked.

"What do we have going on?" Gregg asked.

"A little socializing over breakfast," he teased.

"Hell, Maz, it's been so long since you socialized with anyone other than your boat, I doubt you know how to," Gregg announced loudly.

"Well, that's a pretty shitty way of greeting someone, Gregg," Kelli piped up to defend the captain.

"Just teasing you, old man." Gregg slapped him on the back and almost knocked the wind out of him.

"Young man, I watched yar mother wipe your fat ass when ya were a kid. I know more stories than I doubt ya want shared with such a fine lady like Kelli, so I suggest ya pipe down or better yet, leave."

"Hey, just kidding. How you feeling, Kelli? Anything new at the mansion?"

"Physically fine. Overwhelmed in general. Going to be a slow process. Trying to figure out how I'm going to accomplish what needs to be done. Have the police had any leads on who attacked me the other night?"

Gregg shifted while he stood next to the table as though waiting for an invitation to join them. Sam had known Gregg and his no good father all of his life and didn't trust either one.

Gregg's father, Chuck, had been the chief of police until shamefully discharged. Chuck got into the wrong crowd politically and took bribes under the table to keep silent about things that happened which would affect rich townies and politicians.

Chuck, a local boy, had worked his way up the ranks to achieve the highest position on the force. He was involved in more civic activities than most, giving freely of his time to the community. It was quite the scandal for this small town. A high ranking public servant had never before been released from duties. No one could figure out what caused him to flip from a wonderful public servant to accepting hush money.

In court it was proven he'd received more than five-hundred-thousand dollars to make sure certain politicians and dignitaries were never arrested for actions that might have caused political scandals. He plea bargained and received seven years in prison, unlike others who would have received twenty years easy.

Peers and neighbors speculated and gossiped about the disgrace. He was humiliated. After he got out of prison, Chuck never returned to Manomet. He deserted his wife and son, emotionally and financially.

Sam pitied Gregg when he was a teenager, so he gave him odd jobs after school and on weekends to help his mother make ends meet. From Gregg's comments back then, it was obvious he resented his friends' freedom while he worked to support the family. And worse, he'd been abandoned by a father he adored.

He reckoned that was the turning point of a young man with great potential who now harbored a lifetime of anger and estrangement. He was proud when Gregg joined the police force, against odds, hoping to someday fill his father's position and reinstate the family's good name.

"Hate to report there's no evidence anyone, other than you, was in the house. The case is closed at this point, unless some new evidence crops up."

"Closed? You've got to be kidding me. Well, that's great. I get assaulted and the police department drops it. How can that be?"

"We can't pursue a case where there're no witnesses or evidence. Wish I could inform you differently."

"Hey, Officer Scott. The usual?" the cute waitress flirted.

"Black coffee today, Becky. Thanks. You know, Kelli, I hate to be the one to tell you, but you're probably better off to sell and move on with your life. Just an old friend with an opinion."

Gregg's presence had already exceeded Sam's tolerance level. The more the man talked or bull shitted, the more his blood pressure rose, something he didn't need after the bypass ten years ago.

Kelli balked and shook her head. "I can't tell you how many scenarios I've played out, that being one. But you know Hattie wanted me to keep the property."

"Yeah, but that's not realistic. It's going to cost a fortune. Where in the world you going to come up with that kind of money? And once you get it restored, how you going to afford to keep up the maintenance, taxes, repairs? Sure, the old girl's a beauty, but upkeep will be a financial nightmare."

"Don't you think I know all this? I've gone over all the scenarios a million times. Thanks for your confidence in me, Gregg."

Sam listened to their exchange. It was everything for him to not jump over the table and punch Gregg in his flappin' mouth, but he refrained. Gregg would hang himself in Kelli's eyes eventually anyway.

"Kelli is entitled to make her own decisions," he finally interjected. "We need to support her, not place negative ideas in her mind."

"I'm not negative. I'm realistic and only thinking of her welfare. There're a lot of people in this village that think the old eyesore should be torn down and, quite frankly, they don't care if it's condominiums or what. They just want it down."

"Oh, that's great. So now, I not only have my old friend against the renovation but the whole damn village," Kelli replied loudly.

"Kelli, there's a lot of people in favor of restoring the old lady, so take what Gregg said with a grain of salt. He's spewing his opinion, not others."

The waitress' timing couldn't have been better. She delivered the food which distracted the heated conversation.

He seethed, not a good thing for a man his age and heart condition. How dare Gregg try to persuade Kelli to sell or tear down the house. There was no way he'd let that happen.

Hattie's soul was honor.

CHAPTER 16

Kelli's breath caught while she consumed the view from the widow's walk. Fresh air filled her lungs. Descriptions couldn't portray hues of the sky and sea merged as one or the lush green tops of the dancing trees which overflowed with chickadees and whip-o-wills who chirped melodies. It was tranquility at its best.

She envisioned how a bird felt flying above the trees, gathering views from afar. Fishing and pleasure boats, even tankers, whisked through azure waters, unaware of her presence on the widow's walk. Barges with tugboats came and went from the Cape Cod Canal.

So, this was where it was rumored Belinda Eldridge, in a red dress, paced at night while she waited for her beloved, Joshua, to return from sea. She was chilled to the bone even though it was almost eighty degrees with a fully engaged sun.

According to locals, Belinda fell off the bluff to her death on Manomet Beach after a confrontation with her father over her lover. Who knew what the real truth was after so many years, but every occupant of the mansion over decades swore Belinda haunted the house. She walked the halls, crying, and paced the widow's walk on nights with a full moon.

The neighbor next door, Lynn, stopped by this morning, reintroduced herself, and dropped off a lobster salad. Now almost seventy, she'd lived next to Hattie for at least fifteen years since she inherited the cottage from her father. Dwarfed by the mansion, it had been well maintained and nicely landscaped.

While not in the mood to socialize, she graciously accepted the salad and sat with Lynn for a few minutes. Before she left, Lynn handed her an envelope which contained a wrinkled handwritten paper from a previous tenant who asked she pass it on to Hattie's family. The tenant indicated the family would understand its contents.

She pulled out the envelope she'd tucked in her back pocket. Had Lynn read it? The school paper was white and lined in blue, the ink black and neatly cursive.

A Victorian Dowager

There is an elderly lady
who has lived by the ocean
for over a century.
Once the epitome of elegance,
she won the admiration of all
with her noble mien.
Time has been cruel;
her fine laces are tattered.
She has been stripped of her jewels
and Great Danes have gnawed on her newels.
History whispers through her halls,
while raccoons bumble down the steep service
stairs
to raid the refrigerator.
Black dogs howl with sirens,
and bay at the strangers
who have the temerity to approach
her peeling front doors.
Locals fear those doors;
they point, and shudder,

recounting tales of scarlet-gowned apparitions
who attempt to push unwanted visitors
to their doom
at the foot of the gracious grand staircase.
Wide-eyed witnesses relate
how a shadow sits by the window
of the master suite
waiting, watching
for a captain who will never return,
though the scent of his pipe
yet lingers.
Two policemen were driven off the third floor
by a disembodied voice shouting "Get Out!"
from the thick dark.
One resident tells
of a young girl in a calico dress
who wanders across the front lawn
with a white kitten,
and disappears.
Hearsay and rumor are poison-mawed.
I see different visions,
Days when the mansion
was bright with life,
and every window glowed
with the warmth of the fireplace beyond,
before she was shorn of the tiara
of her widow's walk that views the ocean.
I love her cracked walls,
the shabby opulence of her scrolled trim,
the romances and tragedies
that she has witnessed
through fifteen decades.
I grudge time, and its helpmate, decay.

Every chunk of plaster that rainwater bears crashing
to the broad pine planks of the floor.
But we are poor
and can only sit in her high ceilinged rooms
dreaming of the untold wealth
That would restore this Victorian dowager
to her former glories.

Tears flowed when she reread the poem. The author had focused on points truly relevant to the old beauty.

She'd always been curious about spirits and fully believed when one left this plane they'd travel to another. After her husband's death, she came across an article that said immediately after death six ounces leaves the body, that being the weight of the deceased's soul. She embraced the after-life theory, unable to bear the thought she'd never see Steve, Hattie, or Blake again.

If she were a revisited spirit, this spot would be special. She'd do whatever it took to bring her beloved husband back. If strolling the widow's walk or howling at a full moon worked, she'd be up there every night. If she could have just one more day with him to find out what really happened. More than anything, she needed the reassurance he had loved her enough he had tried to fix the mess he'd created.

It was one thing to be on the widow's walk during the day with full sunlight. Nighttime would be a suicide wish.

CHAPTER 17

The short flight from Hilton Head to Plymouth's municipal airport on BKC's private jet allotted Rod time to evaluate what transpired during his four hour visit to his parents' home.

Would the relationship between his dad and him ever change? Probably not. Since the day Rodney Kesson, IV was born, his father had expectations for him to follow in the footsteps of four paternal generations.

All overachievers, his grandfathers started companies, acquired real estate, and built empires one property at a time. Those assets were passed on to the next generation, who was expected to enhance it more by diversifying real estate, acquiring faltering companies and rebuilding, selling at huge profits.

Each progeny did their part and increased the family's wealth. His father's eccentric, unconventional, and innovative ideas boosted the financial worth of the businesses to billions. Now, he was expected to follow in the same footsteps to grow the wealth more. To make matters worse, his father constantly threw in reminders there wasn't a grandchild to continue the family tradition. It was his heritage. The Kesson legacy must persevere.

He'd never been allowed to be who *he* chose to be, carefree and an unencumbered soul. Instead, it was all about making his father proud, earning money, and being at the top of his game. And now he had disappointed his father—again.

Screw it. This time he was doing it his way. It was time for him to stand up and be the man he knew he could be. But why now? He could have stood his ground on many projects.

Without a doubt it was because of Kelli. Not only was he physically attracted to her, but Kelli's strong affection for the mansion had piqued his interest. Her perception and commitment was unyielding and passionate. Sympathetic for what she'd endured with her husband's death and bankruptcy, he applauded and respected her unselfishness to restore the house against all odds.

Jesus, maybe he had become a softie in his old age. No doubt, there was an undeniable chemistry. With mind and body, a man couldn't fake that type of attraction. If she challenged him mentally, well, that was a plus.

It was odd, but in the short time since he had met her he couldn't seem to get enough of her. He wanted to know everything about her. He craved to touch her and was curious if she felt the same magnetism. If she did, she hid it well behind her attitude. He loved how she folded her arms across her chest, her unpredictability. Their push-pull relationship intrigued him.

"Mr. Kesson. We're beginning our descent into Plymouth. Weather is seventy-eight degrees, partly cloudy. We should be on the ground in about fifteen minutes."

His train of thought was disrupted by the pilot's announcement. The part he hated about flying was the jolt when the tires slammed against the tarmac and screeched to a halt. It escaped him this time, deep in thought about that woman.

He snatched his leather briefcase and matching monogrammed overnight bag, which he didn't need thanks to his father. He disembarked and got into the black limousine which was parked at the end of the stairs.

He was on the verge of a headache. He settled back in the plush seat. The driver didn't bother to strike up a conversation for which he was grateful. He wasn't in the mood for shooting the breeze today. He had a lot on his mind.

The driver delivered him to his motor coach. He tossed in his stuff and grabbed the keys to his Denali. No need to waste time. He had tough negotiations ahead—and a mission. Now, he needed to execute them.

It took seven minutes from his motor coach to the Manomet Mansion. The route was picturesque, a two-lane winding road with mature trees on each side. Cottages and large estates dotted the countryside and occasionally allowed a glimpse of the bay through the maples, cedars, birch, and beech trees. Homes with slate siding had turned grey from years of sea salt and harsh winters.

One house he was particularly fond of was located on a single-lane street hidden amongst the flora. The two-story house sat on the bluff and was almost concealed by a white pergola and fence where an abundance of roses, clematis, and wisteria trailed up the side and cascaded over the top. The three-sided wrap-around porch was surrounded by blue hydrangeas, rhododendrons, and assortment of perennials.

His home on Hilton Head was totally different and resembled more a coastal contemporary on the beach, encased in floor to ceiling glass to catch every view of the beach. It was a gated community for security, and he had his own pier for his speed boat and yacht.

Still, he'd found Pine Hills, south of Plymouth Beach, extraordinary with its hidden population throughout undeveloped hilly and forested areas, crystal clear glacial kettle ponds everywhere.

Kelli's Jeep was parked at the back of the property. He wrung his hands as he approached the sloped porch. It was an ideal summer day, seventy-three degrees with a prevailing southwest summer wind. Would she be receptive to his idea?

It would been a great day to be on his yacht traversing around Nantucket Sound or Island instead of facing a financial battle with a valiant-willed baroness.

He rapped on the open front door, smarting knuckles that had endured little physical labor. All his vigor had been spent on mental economic games. No one answered. Kelli should have been there since her vehicle was parked outside.

"Hello. Anyone home?" he yelled.

No answer.

"Kelli, you here?"

Still no answer.

He slowly squeezed through the massive door and stepped into the vestibule, then into the foyer. He cast a brief look into the parlor on the right, then entered the combination parlor and dining room on the left. Kelli wasn't in either location. He continued through the dining room to a hall with a short, rounded hobbit door. The unusual design made him wonder what was behind the hatch.

"Hello? Kelli?" he shouted from the hallway.

No answer.

He ascended the back servants' staircase, amazed the baluster and spindles matched the main staircase, even though a smaller scale and spindles were brown. At the top landing, he stopped.

"Kelli?"

Again, no response.

Am I overstepping my bounds going through her house? Why isn't she answering? Has something happened to her? Genuine concern surfaced.

He moved onward through each room. He stopped briefly to peek and found less ornate and smaller fireplaces than downstairs. Peeling wallpaper, crumbled and missing plaster exposed horse hair insulation in the walls and fourteen-foot ceilings.

He was astounded the intricate moldings and medallions on the ceilings were intact, given the condition of the walls. A construction guru, he surmised the house suffered damage not only from the leaking roof but variances in temperature, probably not heated during harsh winters.

The rooms became larger and fireplaces more embellished toward the front of the house which indicated the back was reserved for many servants back in the day. Apparently, there'd been a serious water problem with a second floor bath. Floor boards were missing. If someone didn't know about that spot, they'd easily tumble to the first floor.

He was stunned at the condition and what it'd require to restore, but it had mystic charm and was a strong home. He understood now why Kelli and her aunt had been so impassioned with the house.

"Kelli, you here?" he called out louder.

No response.

He approached the northeast front room and found a blow-up bed, cooler, flashlight, and empty water bottles along the wall. A small suitcase sat on an antique table along with a prescription bottle.

Is she staying in the house? Without electricity and other utilities? No way.

When he returned to the hallway, a drawing on the wall in a small room on the left caught his attention. He studied it. What did it represent? Was it a path of life for children since it started with a small brown house on a grassy knoll? Children of various nationalities in native costumes walked the path, some with balloons and flags. Others pulled a wagon and were followed by a turtle. Had this been a child's nursery? Why didn't any of the kids have noses or smiles? Nippy coolness tickled his back.

Quarters on the south side were identical in disrepair and size. He ran into another set of stairs at the back of the house which led to a third floor, its steps narrower. The chambers were smaller yet, walls angled to accommodate the unique Mansard roof which defined set-back windows with wooden shutters barely hanging. When he peered out, Cape Cod Bay was visible over the forest and dotted with moored boats.

"Kelli?" he shouted again in frustration.

No answer.

His heart beat quickened. Had there been another incident? Perhaps she left the house unlocked and went with someone? Officer Scott?

When he reached the front of the house, he discovered a third set of illuminated stairs. He climbed the short set to find an opening in the roof; a hatch on its side. Blinded by brilliant sunlight, he shielded his eyes with his hand. He stuck out his head and moved onto the roof.

He'd had a fear of heights from childhood. At a carnival, he was forced on a ride that descended straight down and dropped at a high rate of speed. He wet his pants and vomited, which embarrassed him in front of his friends.

Kelli was perched on the fractured shingles, bare legs crossed, head resting on her knees. She obviously hadn't heard him. She hadn't moved.

He cautiously climbed next to her; his equilibrium spinning. Vertigo consumed him. He might vomit if he glanced down. God, he prayed he didn't.

CHAPTER 18

Startled, Kelli twisted her torso and stared at Rod wide-eyed. "What in the hell are you doing here?" She wiped wetness from her cheek.

"The question is, what are you doing up here alone?"

"It's my house. I can do whatever I want and if I want to sit up here, I can. I don't need anyone's permission, especially yours."

"You know, Kelli, I don't have to be the adversary here. Actually, I need to talk to you about the offer."

"I heard your offer and I gave you my answer. What else is there to discuss?"

"If you'll come down off the roof, we can talk about this in a civilized manner. This isn't the place to chat about business. So, why are you up here anyway?"

She stared toward the ocean. "I wanted to see the widow's walk. It's dazzling, peaceful, serene. A perfect place for meditation."

"Sure, it's all those things, but it's also hazardous. The railing and shingles are loose. Let me help you down."

"I can get myself down, thank you. Just give me a few minutes. I'll meet you in the parlor."

"Okay, but please be careful. If you have an accident, the first person they'll come looking for is me," he said jokingly.

She didn't reply.

Even though she crawled carefully, she scratched her bare knees on the cracked shingles. She missed the first step when she backed down into the stairway. Sunglasses didn't help her eyes adjust from brightness to darkness.

Rod sat in the parlor on a wobbly Victorian chair, legs crossed. She plopped on an antique wing back, breathless, hot, and dizzy. She wasn't sure if it was due to the change in altitude or his presence.

"Look, I'm not trying to be a bitch, but this is a waste of your time and mine. I haven't had time to consult with my financial advisors about your offer, but it won't change my decision."

"Maybe you should listen for a change and give me a chance to explain."

"Okay." She shook her head, disgusted, and crossed her arms. "The floor's yours."

"I've just returned from headquarters in South Carolina. I came to offer five million dollars. That's our final offer."

"Five million dollars, huh?" Sweat dripped down her neck and onto her tee shirt. Her legs vibrated nervously.

"Yes. That's the limit. Final offer."

"Wow, that's a lot of money." She was taken back and stunned. "Wish I could accept."

"So...how can you make an intelligent decision and turn this down without serious consideration and consultation with professionals? This is an extraordinary once in a lifetime offer." He shifted in his chair. "No one would come remotely close to an offer of this magnitude. Plus, it's a cash offer. We write you a check and you walk away. How can you ignore pecuniary security for you and your family? Are you playing hard ball or what?"

She paused momentarily and fidgeted with her nails. "Nope. No hard ball. You don't get it, do you? There's no amount of money that can make me part with this property. I've had serious time to evaluate everything that's happened to me and my family and what this house meant to my Auntie.

"There's got to be a damn good reason why she was adamant I keep this property regardless of the difficulties I'd face. Do I understand what that means? No. Do I know how hard this is going to be? Yes. But one thing I unequivocally know is what my heart tells me. This house is not going to be destroyed while I'm alive."

For the first time, with eyes riveted, she examined him from top to bottom. He was a handsome, smart, and driven man. Maybe he wasn't the enemy? Was she so exhausted from turmoil her guard was down?

He got out of his chair and sat next to her. When he accidentally bumped her, a shiver slinked up and down her backbone. She missed a man's touch, and for whatever reason, his touch affected her.

When he got excited, his southern drawl was more profound. His eyebrows stayed hiked. His lips tightened when anxious; he'd cross his legs and dangle the foot on top.

"Take time to give this serious consideration. Your financial advisor can show you options on what that amount of money could grow to. You could diversify into various sectors with low risk and live off the interest alone, keeping the principal intact for your son and granddaughters. With five mil, you could invest in muni bonds and live comfortably the rest of your life. Maybe you should think about it from that angle?"

"Thanks, but I'm whipped…emotionally and physically. Tired of everything and everyone right now. Honestly, I'm overwhelmed. I need time to myself to sort through all of this."

"I certainly understand and who wouldn't with this situation? Still, there's one thing you should give serious consideration."

"And what might that be?"

"If you absolutely will not sell to my company, perhaps there are other possible business alternatives you might consider."

What in the world is he trying to do? Confuse me? Is that why he went to South Carolina? To work out a plan of attack with his father?

"I know you don't have the money to restore this house. Perhaps it could be moved to another location on the property. Our corporation would foot the bill and cost of renovations. And give you cash to boot for the land. Would you consider that?"

"Please, don't throw another option at me right now. One minute you're offering me five million. Now you want to move the house and subdivide the land?"

The wind whistled through the house. She shut the double French doors.

"You're throwing all this shit at me so fast, I can't comprehend it. With all that's at stake, I'll seek professional advice, if I decide I'm interested, which I'm not right now. I'm trying to uncomplicate my life...not complicate it, which is exactly what you're trying to do."

"Why don't you let me take you to dinner. Give me an opportunity to discuss this angle. At least, hear me out. Know what your choices are, so you can make an intelligent decision and pass options on to your professional advisors."

"Are you saying I'm not intelligent?"

"No, not at all. I'm just saying there's a lot at stake for you and your family. You need to hear me out, have your financial people consider the options and advise you. Be prudent."

He took a deep breath. "You have nothing to lose and everything to gain. You'd still own the house. It'd get restored, and you'd get cash to boot. Where else you going to get an offer like that? Have dinner with me, please."

"Okay, okay, I'll do dinner. But only if you agree to leave me alone after that. I'm tired of you badgering me. I'm friggin tired of everyone hounding me, hitting me over the head, trying to scare me. I want to be left alone. Deal?"

"Deal. I'll pick you up at six. We'll have dinner on my yacht where it's private and we can talk without distractions."

"Dinner on your yacht," she repeated sarcastically laughing. "This should be interesting."

~ ~ ~

She hadn't felt this flustered since the first time she went out on a date when she was fifteen. She hadn't brought that many clothes with her, but everything she tried on didn't look good. She'd try on one outfit, then quickly take it off and try on another.

Her lipstick was not pink enough. Her hair was flat. She wanted it bouncy.

Why was she so concerned with looking attractive to impress the man who grabbed her attention so quickly? But, he was trying to take away the only thing she owned. How could she have such conflicting emotions? What was wrong with her?

She had only one job to do. When she got on that boat, in no uncertain terms would she agree to sell the mansion.

CHAPTER 19

Rod promptly picked up Kelli at six in his black Mercedes convertible. He'd lingered in the hot shower contemplating his tactical approach and various financial possibilities. Those thoughts were interrupted easily when he envisioned what she might look like tonight.

His father had called. He purposely let the message go to voice mail, not inclined to listen to another round of ranting.

"So, think we can start over?" he broke the silence when he helped her into the low-lying car and shut the door. "Hi, my name is Rod," he teased when he pulled out of the driveway.

She grinned faintly but appeared tired. Her hair was loose around her face, curly enough to emphasize her distinct petite features and clear complexion. Shimmering sapphire eye shadow accented her large blue orbs and complemented her azure cotton dress. He wondered if the pale emerald sea glass necklace and matching dangling earrings were from a local artist or if she'd made them. A loosely knit white sweater was draped over one arm, along with a small clutch.

Distracted with her next to him, he almost missed a stop sign at the busiest intersection in Manomet.

"Gee, if I didn't know better I'd surmise you're a little nervous tonight," she said.

"My, you've found me out. You actually have a sense of humor."

"Not really. Don't try to get on my good side. I don't have one," she teased.

She's not only attractive, but witty. Maybe we share a light side?

"I'm only here because of Auntie and my family," she continued. "Plus, it's been a while since I've had a real meal. I might as well take advantage of you."

You? Take advantage of me?

She was interesting. He'd love to respond with a clever remark with sexual undertones to see her response, but figured better. He'd worked hard to get this far with her; he didn't want to scare her away now. It was difficult to keep his eyes on the road. He wanted to take in every movement she made.

Fifteen minutes was all it took from Manomet to Brewers Boat Yard in Plymouth. She was out of the car before he could assist, probably not used to men with southern manners.

Will she be impressed with my yacht?

Entry to the boardwalk was required by a plastic card only given to members. The yacht was docked in the last slip and moored sideways since it was one-hundred-feet long and three stories high towering over the others.

His hefty security guard paced in front of the craft to ensure no one attempted to board. Individuals who were famous and wealthy like the Kesson family were surefire prey for advantage seekers, idiots who wanted their picture taken on a celebrity's yacht, or someone who might consider kidnapping for ransom.

Instead of white plastic buoys attached to the sides to prevent scraping, the boat yard installed special dock bumpers in case waves got rough behind the large stone wall protecting the marina.

They sauntered down the dock. He instinctively grabbed her arm and pulled her close to prevent her from tripping over a warped board, not thinking of the repercussions from the physical touch. The heat from her body was soothing; it'd been a while. He missed a woman's touch.

CHAPTER 20

Unbelievable. The last thing Kelli envisioned herself doing would be boarding a yacht, especially given her dire financial situation. And with an extremely handsome and wealthy man.

Why did I fall into this trap, stupid? What was I thinking? This man isn't interested in me. He's only interested in the mansion. Get a reality check.

"Ma'am, let me help you," a steward in a white suit asked, grabbing her hand.

She stepped from the rocking dock to the boat. Rod stayed behind and chatted with a crew member to give lengthy instructions, using his hands as emphasis.

"Kelli, let's go to stern and get settled."

His announcement startled her. He extended his hand for support. She was surprised at its strength, yet it was warm and gentle. Realization set in she hadn't held another man's hand since her husband died. A hand wasn't all she hadn't held. They walked along the outside of the boat to the canopied outdoor area.

"Ma'am, may I get you something to drink?" a short man inquired, also uniformed in white.

"Sure. What're my choices?"

"Mr. Kesson stocks a full bar, so I'm sure he'll have whatever you desire."

"Well then, how about a rum, diet Coke with a lime, please. Make that a tall with not much ice."

"Yes, ma'am." He turned and walked away into the cabin.

The view was astonishing. Rod's yacht was probably twenty times larger than any boat docked at the marina.

Seagulls glided aimlessly and targeted leftovers from fishing vessels or boaters feeding from docked vessels. It was a perfect evening, no wind, few clouds, and calm seas. Were they staying at the marina or taking the boat out, which would've been a thrill, even though she hesitated being alone with a man she didn't know. *What if he tries to harm me? No one knows where I am. Maybe he was behind the attack at the mansion?* Her belly wrenched. Had she made a terrible mistake?

"Is Sy getting you a drink?" Rod asked politely.

"Yes, he is. Thanks." Why had her heartbeat quickened and she was jittery, symptoms of hypoglycemia? Had she eaten enough today?

He sat next to her, even though six teak chairs were around the glossy, slick handcrafted table. If a bird had tried to land, it'd slide off. She chuckled at the image.

Rumblings and vibrations caught her off-guard. She grabbed the arm on the chair. The yacht moved leisurely sideways from the dock, no captain in sight.

"I hope you're on no particular timeframe. Thought we'd take the boat out. If we're lucky we might catch a peek at seals or right whales. It's a beauty out there today."

"No. No timeframe," she responded nervously. "Your boat is incredible. I've never been on anything like this." Even if she didn't want to cruise alone with this stranger, she had to admit she was enthralled to go out into the bay on a boat of this magnitude. It was probably a once in a lifetime chance to see how the wealthy lived. She could adjust her lifestyle to accommodate this.

"Thanks. It's a Hatteras one hundred Raised Pilothouse…newest on the market. Don't think there's a better way to evaluate a business deal than when you're relaxed in an out-of-the-office environment," he teased.

"Out-of-the-office environment, huh? I certainly would consider this more than that. It's unlike any office I've ever seen."

"My father discovered decades ago if you get your clients relaxed, it's much easier to work out a deal. Golf courses and fishing work the same way."

"So, you're trying to get me, your client, relaxed? Is that it?" The tone in her voice elevated.

"Now, don't take offense to what I said right off the bat, Kelli. I'm trying to make this convenient and easy as possible."

"I appreciate the consideration, but somehow I get the impression I'm going to be stuck on this yacht until we reach some type of compromise?" Surprised at her own light heartedness, she touched her legs that shook under the table. "Is that why you use boats? To capture your clientele until they give in? Or throw them overboard if they don't?"

"My, I love your Manomet sense of humor. I'm impressed."

"Don't be. It doesn't last long."

The waiter reappeared and placed two drinks on the table along with blue linen napkins, a Mikasa bowl filled with jumbo iced shrimp, cocktail sauce, and lemon slices. He swayed slightly while the vessel cruised out to sea.

"Thank you," she said.

"My pleasure, ma'am. I'll be back shortly with the next course."

Rod sipped his drink. The lowering sun amplified the smile lines around his eyes and mouth and displayed slightly weathered skin and heavy eyebrows. He flipped on a pair of Versace sunglasses. He crossed his muscled legs which exposed untarnished docksiders.

"I understand your commitment to your deceased aunt to honor her final wishes. I don't think you've any idea what the cost would be to restore. Not only monetarily for the restoration, but emotionally for you to try and maintain the mansion."

She raised her index finger.

"Now wait," he said. "Let me explain before you interrupt. I've been involved in acquiring land and developing condominium projects with my dad since high school. I know what it takes to restore properties, especially ones that have been neglected. Without our financial assistance, I don't think it's possible for you to pull this off."

"You think I don't understand finances and what this involves? You're wrong. I'm college educated and believe me, I've thought about this from every angle. It's hard for me to sleep nights since I arrived in town and saw the condition of the house."

"I can imagine given what's happened in the past."

She squared her back against the wooden slats. "What do you know about my past?" Why was she so quickly agitated?

"It's part of my business to do my homework on prospective clients."

"I'm not a prospective client. I've told you that."

"Now, let's not get our dander up. Let's try to work through this together, shall we? I'm not the enemy." He placed his hand on her arm.

Its warmth sent searing stimulating waves throughout her body. She welcomed his touch but automatically raised her emotional wall.

"I'm not sure who's the enemy anymore. Okay, you have my attention."

"If you won't sell the mansion and property to me outright, I propose we become business partners. My firm, BKC Properties, would become the majority stockholder in a partnership where we'd move the mansion from the present location to the edge of the acreage, renovate, restore, and financially maintain the mansion."

He faced her and leaned into her. "Terms of the partnership would allow you to live in the house rent free for your lifetime. Maintenance expenses would be paid through the partnership. We'd have to do due diligence on this type of scenario, but I think it's doable. We both win. You get to keep the house on the property; we get to use the rest of the land for development. Maybe we'll call the condominium units The Mansions," he teased.

"After you're deceased, your son and his family will own control over your interest, so it stays in your family. The descendants can pass it down. I don't see how a situation could get any better than this."

She focused on what he described and captured every word. Yes, she understood how partnerships worked. She should ask pertinent questions, but suddenly, her mind went void. She was studying his mannerisms, the way his mouth curled up, his smile. The fact he had made eye contact through the sunglasses and didn't look away.

"Partnership, huh? And you want majority interest? This is something to be drawn up by your legal team and presented to my accountant and attorney for review. Don't know I would give you majority interest. Moving the house will probably be the deal breaker though. The location is what the house is about…and memories. Anything that's changed will destroy that."

She was enthralled in the conversation and being close to him, so she hadn't noticed the distance the yacht had cruised into the bay until she looked up. The shoreline had shrunk as the sun bore down on her bare legs, warming them.

Multi-colored scraped buoys bobbed on the silken surface of the water, lobster pots dangled far below. Fishermen labored over their pots as they lugged crustaceans, crabs, and a few small fish into their boats which were pint-sized in comparison to the yacht. People stared.

The red mile marker bellowed its warning. Was it a sign for her too?

Memories surged back as though on Auntie's boat. They'd tender to the motorboat with a mess of blues caught earlier to put in the bait bags. At first, she couldn't bear to chop off their heads and wrap them in cheesecloth and stick in the lobster pot. The odor of decayed fish made her want to wretch.

It became easier over time. Auntie was thrilled to not only have her on the boat but taught her a skill not learned in textbooks. Auntie struggled with MS and it got worse the older she got, but it never stopped her daily routine of checking lobster pots, unless the weather didn't cooperate. She had a residential license which allowed ten traps. She loved her lobster, the boat, the work, and the bay.

Rock crabs were one of Auntie's favorites but became too much work when she got older. She hated how fresh fish and lobster peered at her when she threw them in a pot of boiling water. That was an ongoing joke between them. Auntie loved fresh bluefish grilled with a mayonnaise herb basting. Captain Maz teased her if he tried to cook a bluefish, it'd taste like an old sneaker. He always chopped it up for bait.

"Hello? You still with me?" Rod touched her arm.

"Sorry. Lobster pots reminded me of Auntie. I pulled traps with her when I visited."

"Really? Bet that was fun."

"And have you ever pulled one up?"

"No, can't say I have, but believe me, I can do anything I set my mind to."

"Oh, I'm sure you can."

"So, what do you think about my proposal?"

"I think it sounds too good to be true. Not sure it's doable. Moving the house probably won't work. Can't imagine the house sitting anywhere other than where it is. Just too many memories."

"There's a lot of prime land on the acreage where it could be relocated. I could have my architects draw up an illustration, so you can see it on paper. Would that help?"

"I don't know." She sighed. "There's so much to consider. Means we'd be working together. If we're in a partnership, I'd have to make decisions jointly with you where you'd want to dictate what's going to be done. Too many variables. No one will control me again. Ever."

"I totally understand your dilemma and can only imagine how overwhelmed you are with all of this. So, let's look at the two options. You can take the five mil and run.

"Or, I can get my attorneys and engineers to draw up a proposal. We can meet again and review it in great detail. If you want, I'll fly my attorney and engineer in. We'll meet with whoever you want and answer questions. Actually, I'll do something we typically don't do. We'll pick up all of your team's costs for them to review the proposal. Won't cost you a dime to hear me out."

She toyed with the beveled glass that had contained the drink she consumed too quickly. "Guess all I can do is look at the situation, even though I'm not sure either will work. But, for my peace of mind, I'm willing to listen. God knows, I don't have the money to do it myself."

"Deal then?" He stuck out his hand.

Her hand connected with his which sent waves throughout her body. "I'm not saying deal. I'm only saying I'll check it out."

He smiled suggestively, melting her insides. Or, was he playing her for a fool? Was the drink purposely loaded to make her agree to a partnership?

She straightened her shoulders. He had no idea who he was dealing with.

~ ~ ~

Tonight's experience would be one Kelli wouldn't forget for several reasons. For the first time since her husband's death, she felt oddly secure with Rod Kesson. She doubted she'd ever be on a yacht of that magnitude again.

She fought embracing the fact she found him appealing. Was it his persona? Wealth? His occasional touch to her arm or back every chance he got?

His body was toasty, something she'd missed for the last five years. When he leaned into her, he transmitted an undercurrent of emotions. His sensuous cologne captured her senses. He should have been in an Old Spice commercial; she loved that smell on him.

While astonished with the opulent yacht and obvious wealth, that didn't appeal to her. If anything, it made her wary of his intentions. Rod appeared to have changed in front of her, just like a chameleon. Instead of combative about the house, now he wanted to help restore and pay for it to boot.

But emotionally deep-seated, she worried this was a ploy to break her down, to acquire partial interest now, then screw her out of the remaining interest later. After what happened with her husband, she wasn't sure she'd ever trust another man. Maybe she'd been played enough. He'd offered for her to spend the night on the yacht but she declined, knowing it'd be safer at the mansion.

Do I not trust myself with him? That's ridiculous.

He'd been a gentleman and escorted her back to the mansion, although it was past ten and dark.

"I'll touch base with you tomorrow after I talk to my team," he announced, acting slightly uneasy.

Or was she the one uncomfortable?

"That's fine, but Rod...."

A movement on the widow's walk caught her attention. Was someone on the roof?

CHAPTER 21

Gregg pulled up the gravel driveway. He surveyed the mansion and wheezed. Dust had quickly settled from the slight rain earlier that morning.

Why in the hell would Kelli want to deal with this mess?

He turned off his laptop and slid out of the police cruiser. He readjusted the cumbersome belt that held his police apparatus rarely needed in this peaceful village.

His wet boot slipped when he stepped on the last crooked step. "Kelli?" He rapped on the slightly ajar door.

Footsteps pattered toward him.

"Gregg, how are you?" Kelli greeted.

"Hey there. Fine. Just checkin' to see how you're doing. Haven't talked to you in a few days and happened to be in the neighborhood checking on ole' Buster down the road. Guess he had another fight with the wife, and she called the police again. Never ending those two. After being married for forty years you'd think it'd be a cake walk."

"Come on in. Don't think I know those folks, do I?"

"Doubt it. They moved to town three years ago from the West Coast and all they do is fight. They're both too damn old to be carrying on like this. Adds excitement to my otherwise dreary police duties some days."

"Doubt your duties are dreary, Gregg. Bet there's a lot of excitement in Manomet and Plymouth."

"Sure. Taking home drunks from the bar, arresting people for jay walking, illegal parking at White Horse

Beach. Yeah, my life's pretty exciting. Enough about me. How are you? Been thinking about you."

"Well, that's nice. I'm working upstairs going through some of Hattie's boxes. I've got a couple I could use help moving. Got time?"

"Always have time for you, Kelli." He winked.

Was she encouraging him to stick around? His heart skipped a beat.

He treaded behind her up the back staircase to the second floor then took the short staircase to the third. Her body hadn't changed much over the years. Still slim, trim, and incredibly attractive. She'd aged well. He was sorry she'd lost her husband so tragically. He'd seen his share of car accidents and none were easy to take, even for the first responders.

He was self-conscious he'd let his body go having gained over fifty pounds, most of it flab due to a poor diet of fast food and beer. The only exercise he got was getting in and out of his car at least a dozen times a day or climbing steps to the beach when there was a problem.

They strolled down the long hallway to the front of the house until they arrived at a small room with three windows, each arched in different heights, lending a unique appearance from inside and out.

"Guess Auntie used this for storage throughout the years and maybe the renters stuck stuff up here too. This locked chest is so heavy, I can't budge it. Let me scoot the stuff on top of it on the floor. Can you give me a hand moving it?"

"Here, step aside. Where do you want it?"

"I'm trying to get everything lined up in the hallway, so I can go through one container at a time. All I'm finding so far are piles of paid bills, cancelled checks, old newspapers, coastal magazines, recipe books, probably since the day she was born. Who knows how far back this stuff goes. I swear, I can't imagine why she'd want to keep all this shit."

"Your guess is as good as mine." The vintage brown leather chest was bulky. He flexed his knees and strained. He hoped it didn't tear the hernia he'd been babying to avoid surgery.

"Good Lord. What in the world's in here?"

The trunk thudded when it landed on the warped wooden floor.

"Guess I'll find out soon. Looks like I'll have to pry open the lock. Have no idea where she might have kept the key. If you can help me scoot these other five boxes out here, that'd be a huge help."

"No prob."

The other cartons were a piece of cake compared to the chest, even though the cardboard bottoms had fallen apart. Kelli had done an outstanding job of cleaning up debris throughout the house, organizing boxes and containers to go through in one area on each floor.

He'd been in the mansion shortly after Hattie's death and couldn't believe the pig pen the renters had left and how much furniture they'd absconded with. He figured the entire place would go up in smoke some day since the rubbish posed a fire hazard.

"Gracious, thanks for your help. I'd never got that one moved."

"Glad I was here to help."

"How about some water? It's already heating up in here, and it's not even ten o'clock yet. Guess it's humid from the shower this morning. Can't believe the roof on this ole' place has held up so well.

"There's one place on the second floor where it's leaked and floorboards are missing. Looks like the renters were in the process of repairing the bath, but must have left in a hurry. Maybe the ghosts scared them," she joked.

He cast a brief look around. "They don't make houses like this anymore. What a shame it's gotten in this shape. I don't want to be a naysayer, but you know what you're getting into?"

"Let's go downstairs where it's cooler. Actually, I've got some bottled lemonade. If I remember correctly after all these years, that's one of your favorites."

"Got vodka to go with it?" He smiled playfully.

Her grin was welcoming; her smile gleamed from corner to corner exposing white, straight teeth. He recalled when her mouth was full of metal and how awkward it was to kiss her. He liked awkward. He followed her down two sets of stairs, observing her familiar bounce from younger days and her wonderful cheeks.

"Here you go. Probably not cold enough, but at least, it's wet."

"Wet is good." He inspected the makeshift kitchen. "What happened here?"

"Guess there was a small fire and the renters gutted it. Auntie would be devastated if she knew her beautiful kitchen had been destroyed. Between my memory and the old pictures, I plan to restore like she had it.

"Breaks my heart to think all the years she slaved away in here and now it's gone. There was never a time it wasn't full of homemade baked goods and meals. Her lobster salad was the best, and lemon meringue pie was to die for."

"Yep, she was quite the woman, wasn't she? Fed us many meals and packed our picnic lunches for the beach. Wonderful lady. So, any decisions on what you plan to do?"

She reclined against the exposed wooden wall, irregular lines of white insulation peeked out between the slats. "Between you and me and this is not to be repeated, I've had a couple of offers from Rod Kesson."

"That snake," he hissed.

"He not only made me an unbelievable flat out cash offer, he's also indicated we could go into partnership to fix up the house, but would require moving it. I've got so many options running through my head, I can't even begin to sort them out."

"Don't trust that asshole, Kelli. He'll trick you into doing something you'll regret. Heard he'd purchased lots of land up and down the East Coast and destroyed prime seashore to build condominiums. I wouldn't give him the time of day." His pulse elevated.

"I know. I have my own thoughts about his motives, but on the other hand, I don't have many choices if I want to keep the old family home from being destroyed."

"Maybe there're no recourses because it's meant to be. Perhaps it's time to retire this old lady and take care of yourself for a change."

She turned away and stopped in front of the grimy window in the sunroom. "I don't know. Too many variables right now. I need time to sort through all of this, without emotions, with professional financial and legal advice. Mull over what's best for me and my family."

Without thinking, he shifted next to her. She pivoted. Their eyes locked. He moved closer. His heart palpitated. Could he still be in love with her after all these years? Or was it simply a lack of female companionship for so long?

She swiveled to the side and shifted her gaze to something beyond him. "I have something to show you."

Oh boy! Maybe this was it. He stroked his forehead with the back of his hand. But why had she turned away?

"Follow me."

Anywhere. His mind slipped again.

She dashed to the upstairs bedroom and walked to a timeworn night stand and picked up a plastic container. She opened the lid.

"Do you have any idea what this is?" She exposed a silver nugget the size of a quarter.

He twisted it from side to side, his heart pounded from the run up the stairs. "Where'd you get this?"

"You won't believe it, but I found it on the floor next to my bed yesterday. I have no idea where it came from. The really strange thing is I've swept this floor a few times and it wasn't there before."

He inspected the piece. An avid coin collector since his grandfather taught him at the age of ten, he had a gut idea, but it was highly unlikely.

"I'm not sure. Looks pretty old to me. Wonder if it's a replica and came from Town Brook. Guess people still go down there and sift for stuff."

He'd only seen one of these before at a museum. The *Forest Queen* had wrecked a century and a half ago. The captain confused his lighthouses and ran hard ashore near Pegotty Beach. It was rumored pounds of pure silver ingots were buried along with her amongst the rocks.

So, maybe the rumors were true. Captain Eldridge had stashed treasures in the old mansion after all.

CHAPTER 22

Kelli allowed Gregg to take the specimen to investigate its worthiness but acknowledged it was probably of no significant value.

Shortly after he left, she retreated to the second floor northwest bedroom to investigate a loose board in the closet she'd tripped on yesterday, causing a sizable splinter to lodge in her big toe.

This was one of her favorite rooms with its eight-foot windows on three of its four walls, bright and cheery most days even though the majority of the wallpaper hung loosely. The off-white mantel was crafted on the dainty side unlike the others and was supported by rusty iron brackets versus wood. She pried the floorboard with a screwdriver, wedging her body against the wall for leverage.

An object wrapped in stained yellow paper was underneath the floorboard. She slid her hand between the joists, knowing spiders or other creatures inhabited the space. Her curiosity piqued. Sticky cobwebs clung to her fingers inserted in a space no bigger than the width of four knuckles. Spiders, crickets, and dead bugs affixed themselves. She shook her hand immediately after laying the package on the floor.

She hesitantly uncurled the crumbled paper. She gasped. A miniature Noritake teacup with matching saucer peeked out. She recognized the Shenandoah pattern Auntie had collected and displayed in the built-in china hutch in the dining room.

Not thrilled about inserting her hand into the minute dungeon again, she was curious if anything else was hidden. To her surprise, another poorly wrapped package brushed against her fingers.

Her hands trembled and heart raced with excitement as she reached in. The paper on this parcel was darker stained and tied with a string. When she peeled the paper back, there were two maroon goblets, also collected by Hattie and displayed in the cabinet.

Why in the world would Auntie hide these? Oh my, God.

She unraveled the newspaper from the last parcel, pieces disintegrated from her touch. Shredded around the edges, it was dated eighteen-hundred-sixty-three and displayed an ad for the Charley Brown, a flannel type jacket and original totes.

How ironic was that? Charlie Brown had been the name of Manomet's blue spruce Christmas tree which had been hydraulically spaded from a construction corner in front of the liquor store down the street. They transplanted it on Auntie's corner. Charlie saw one marvelous holiday at his new home but didn't survive the brutal winter and blizzard. How strange to find an ancient clipping with the same name.

Had her finger rubbed against something else when she pulled out the last bundle? She held her breath and closed her eyes. Her hand sunk deeper into the space. Another packet touched her, but could she get her fingers around it?

Determined, she moved in deeper. An old nail tore her skin, but she almost had it. With one final push, she grabbed her prize. She rubbed the cobwebs off her hand and shivered at the nasty bugs attached.

She unfolded the third package. It was by far larger than the others and was fortunate it came out at all. A vintage suede bound book, approximately four by seven, had fallen apart at the seams. She blew on the cover. Dust flew from years of filth. On the brown cover in black ink was one word scribed in elegant calligraphy— Joshua. The skin flaked from the binding. She tenderly cuddled it.

Joshua was Belinda Eldridge's lover. Was this a diary? Why was it hidden in here with delicate glassware?

Auntie had insisted the house contained secrets and someday she'd share them, but Alzheimer's developed too quickly. Was this one of them?

She opened the first page, discolored onion skin shredded on top.

To my dear, Joshua-

> *Today you left me for the sea and my heart is broken. I understand why you had to go, to earn coin so we could be together forever. I already miss our clandestine meetings in our special place on the bluff. My memories will sustain me until you return, even though my heart is torn into many pieces and I can't bear another minute without your loving touch. I will count the days until your return. I love you with all my heart and soul. Please hurry home.*

> *Love you endearingly, Belinda*

Her body shook. The inked words were scribed in neat handwriting, but smeared over years. Even though faded, it was still easy to read. She turned to the next page and carefully handled like it was the Constitution.

To my dear Joshua-

While today is only the second day you have been gone, my heart tells me it has been a lifetime. In great sorrow of your absence, I mounted Rocky and took our favorite trail to Rabbit Pond. I played in the sand and recalled the days we spent frolicking in the water and loving each other, enjoying the serenity of the flowering bushes and flowers. I can't bear to live another day without you. Each day seems like an eternity already. I hope you know how much I love and need you.

Father has been on a rampage again and last night he was violent after consuming too much homemade spirits. He scares me and without you to talk to, I have no one. Mother even seems to be afraid of him. Please hurry home. I need you. I hope your voyage will be swift and safe. I will pray for you every night of my life.

Love you endearingly, Belinda

Her hands quivered while she embraced the tattered book and carefully thumbed through a few pages.

To my dear Joshua–

It's been two weeks since you left my heart and soul, and I think about you constantly and visit our special place every day on the bluff. Yesterday Mother took me to town to shop for clothes for an affair Father is having. I only wear these clothes for my mother and to keep my father happy. Father had a bee at the house, which displeased me greatly. He invited his codfish aristocracy friends, some of which were incredibly rude, some pawing at me like a doll. I hate living like this–my father introducing me to young men as though you don't exist. I can't stand any of them. They aren't like you–kind, sweet, caring, respectful. I can't stand being away from you another minute longer. Hurry home and take me away from this madness. Sometimes I wonder about my father–how he can be so kind one minute and like a devil the next. Since Kent died, he's a changed man. Our house is so full of sorrow. He watches my every movement. Please whisk me away. I love you with all my heart.

Love you endearingly, Belinda

She carefully flipped to the last page of the diary, trying not to disturb the fragmented pages. She sensed she'd disturbed a long, lost message.

To my dear Joshua-

It has now been one hundred and seven days since you have been to sea. I am sick with worry. Father told me the ship you sailed went down in a nor'easter off the coast, but I know he is lying to me. I can feel it in my heart. He would never allow us to be together-he considers all to be below his standards. But I know you're my heart and soul. I have the most wonderful news, Joshua. I am with child. Our child. I thought I was dying of cholera. I could not eat or keep any food down for weeks. My abdomen became plump. I can now feel the baby move, as though butterflies are flitting in my tummy. It's the most remarkable feeling, and this baby keeps me so close to you-it's part of both of us. I have not shared this news with anyone, but fear my mother knows. I'm wearing looser clothes, and can't stand to have a corset bound to me. Please hurry home. Your child and I need and love you. We're going to be a family, Joshua. Everything we dreamed and talked about can come true. We have to be together.

Love you endearingly, Belinda

She placed the book on the floor and backed up to the wall. Dangling wallpaper scraped her arm. Even though the sun shone brightly through each window, coldness filled the air. A mist formed in the corner.

The silhouette slowly became more distinct. It took on human form. An alluring young woman with long, blonde, silky hair stood feet away. Pale perfect skin, cobalt-colored eyes like the deep sea, but watery. Her expression was sad, like lost in time.

"You found my diary and treasured china. I saved those for my daughter," the figure said.

She couldn't answer. She wasn't afraid but welcomed the contact.

The haze shifted from the corner and floated to the floor in front of her. She laid on her side. She was breathtakingly captivating. Every detail from the top of her head to the end of her pink full-length satin gown was exquisite. She hovered in front of Kelli, close enough to touch. She was drawn to the woman's despondent eyes.

"You have to save our home or Joshua will not be able to find me and our baby girl when he returns from the sea. You understand my loss. I understand yours. We are connected through our sorrow of our loved ones we have been separated from. You are the only one who can set me free and bring Joshua home. But beware, you are in grave danger."

The misty figure vanished abruptly.

Her shallow breathing caused lightheadedness; her hands and body were frigid even though eighty-five degrees. An orange and yellow vapor filled the room, highlighted from the impending sunset which streamed through the dirt-encrusted windows.

What time was it? How long had she read the journal? *What's that odor? Smoke?*

CHAPTER 23

"Ten-seventy at Twenty-Nine Manomet Point Road. Occupant is outside. Repeat—occupant is unharmed and outside."

Stunned by the message, Gregg quickly slammed on his brakes and skidded the opposite direction, speeding to the Manomet Mansion. It wasn't the mansion he thought of. It was Kelli.

One block away, the familiar stench of charred wood drifted into the cruiser and up his nostrils, which reminded him of bonfires on the beach. Flashing crimson, silver, and blue lights gleamed through the smoke when he turned into the gravel driveway, screeching to a halt. Even though the lane was long, it was filled with two fire trucks, several squad cars, and a yard of nosey onlookers.

"What happened, Jack?" he shouted.

"Got a fire on the back corner of the house," the firefighter replied while he advanced the hose.

"Anyone injured?"

"No. Only occupant smelled smoke and called in. She's over there." The fireman nodded towards the old tree. "Looks like a small fire."

Kelli was easy to spot in the crowd. Rod Kesson stood next to her.

Gregg darted over and wrapped his arm around her shivering shoulders. "Kelli, what happened? You all right?"

"Yes, I'm fine. But I don't know what happened. I was up in the bedroom. Smoke came up the back stairway.

They think someone deliberately started the fire. What in the hell's going on?"

"I don't know, but the most important thing is you're safe. Guess the fire's small and it's out, but I don't want you staying here tonight." It felt good having his arm around her again like the old days, pulling her close.

Rod watched his every movement.

"No one's running me out of my home. They can knock me in the head and try to burn my house down, but I'm not leaving." Her voice cracked with emotion.

"Here, why don't you sit in my car and get out of this smoke. I'll be right back."

He was amazed she agreed by nodding her head. They sauntered to the car. Rod Kesson followed.

He slammed the door, turned and faced Rod. "Kesson, everything's under control. I'll take care of Kelli. No need for you to stick around. You wouldn't know anything about this fire, would you?"

"That's a stupid question, Officer. Why would I?"

"Other than Kelli, you seem to be the only person in town interested in this property."

"So, I have an interest and I want to burn it down? You're pretty slick mentally, aren't you?"

"I don't have time for this bullshit. This is a police matter. Don't know if we'll find out anything tonight, so I suggest you leave."

"Only on one condition. Kelli comes with me."

"And why in the hell would Kelli want to come with you?"

"Because I'm concerned over her safety, and I have a place she can stay tonight."

"Get the hell out of here, Kesson. I'll worry about Kelli." He strolled over to the fire chief. "Got anything so far, Chief?"

"Not too damn much. Looks like someone lit a small fire with old driftwood at the base of the house in the far right corner which leads to the cellar. Maybe kids playing with matches. It's a damn good thing she was home. Being the wood's this dry, it would've gone up like a torch. She's lucky, that's for sure. Both of them."

"Lucky? Maybe tonight. She can't seem to catch a break."

"We're going to stick around to make sure embers don't re-engage. Fire marshal will come around tomorrow to do his survey, and we'll let you know what we find out. The house's electricity is out of code and damn old. One of the neighbors indicated the new owner has been staying here. Know anything about that?"

"This lady is a long-time friend of mine, Russ. Let me worry about her and where she stays, okay?"

"Gotcha." The heavy fire helmet shifted on the captain's sweaty head.

He walked back to the car to find Kesson leaned over the open door chatting with Kelli. His blood pressure, given his age, overweight, smoking, and non-existent exercising, probably exceeded healthy limits.

"Okay, Kesson. Show's over. You can leave now."

"Not until I know Kelli's going to be safe tonight."

"Kelli, why don't you stay at my house? No one's going to bother you there." He glanced at Rod to see if he got a rise.

"Thanks everyone for the offers, but I really want to be alone tonight. I'll stay at the Blue Spruce, so I can get a good night's rest. I'm exhausted...mentally and physically. I appreciate all the help and the offers though," she responded slowly.

"Well, at least I know you'll be safe with Cheryl and Tom. Ready to go?" he asked.

"I probably should get a couple of things, but I know Cheryl keeps extras and I'll be back tomorrow. I grabbed my purse and cell phone when I ran out of the house. Yes, I'm ready."

He slammed the door, almost catching part of Rod's finger.

Kelli rolled down the window. "Thanks, Rod. I appreciate your concern."

"Sure, Kelli. Take care and if you need anything, here's my card. Call me day or night."

"Thanks," she replied weakly.

Gregg revved the engine of his cruiser and backed out the driveway. He phoned ahead to the Blue Spruce to let them know what had happened and Kelli needed a place to stay even though they were a few minutes away. He glanced at Kelli. She seemed emotionally torn apart.

The owners welcomed her with open arms and already had the porch and inside lights on. Toiletries, robe, and slippers were set out.

She would be safe until tomorrow...until he found out what was going on.

CHAPTER 24

Fatigued, Kelli climbed into the tub in her room at the Blue Spruce Motel to soak away terrible memories and the stench of smoke from the last couple of hours. Tears dribbled down her cheeks when she recalled the events of the fire. Was someone trying to kill her or scare her away? Gregg thought it was a matter of bad coincidences and nothing more. Her gut instinct indicated differently. Or perhaps it was her raw emotions alerting her to be wary.

Am I losing it? Did Belinda warn me of impending danger before the fire?

After a restless night, mentally unable to shut out what happened, she rose early with a plan. She'd go to the Manomet library and research the mansion and its original occupants. She had to start somewhere to sort this out in her mind. That seemed the most logical.

Had the stress of the last five years suddenly caught up with her? Had the anti-depressant drugs accumulated in her system to the point she hallucinated and heard Belinda, a ghost?

As she left the room, she was tempted to survey the fire damage, but couldn't bear to see where someone had been malicious, regardless of whether it was against her or her home.

She walked to the Manomet Branch Library which was on Strand Avenue, a block from the motel. The single floor dwelling had two sections with outside doors, and she surmised it'd been a bank once since it had a drive-up window. She wasn't sure which door to use.

She tingled with excitement and nervousness, hoping research might shed light on the past.

"May I help you, ma'am?" a lady in her mid-sixties inquired from behind the chest-high counter loaded with pens, bookmarks, and posters taped to the front advertising an upcoming Family Story Time.

"Yes, as a matter of fact you can. I'm Kelli Goddard. I own the Manomet Mansion around the corner. I'd like to look at anything you might have about the mansion and the Eldridges."

"My oh my, so nice to meet you, Mrs. Goddard. I have to tell you, we all loved Hattie and were so sad to hear she passed. She was a true patron of this community. I think she's the one who donated the book over there with original handwritten facts and letters from Manomet residents over the years.

"A true community servant for Manomet, serving precincts six and seven, the steering committee, and on the board here at one time. She instituted thought provoking ideas where others never would and—"

"Sorry to interrupt and I appreciate the kind words. I'd love to chat another time, but I'm on a tight agenda today. If you wouldn't mind showing me the way, I would certainly appreciate it."

"Sorry. I get carried away sometimes. By all means, follow me."

Two teenagers giggled while they played on computers under the four windows with an arched topper. Others sat around with iPads, so she assumed the library had Wi-Fi.

Anxiously, she followed the lady who strolled at a snail's pace. They passed corridor after corridor of books from floor to ceiling. Some books showed their age by their covers. Maybe the library had a small staff and was funded or relied on volunteers and donations to keep it viable?

The section for children caught her eye, decorated in bold colors with a bright red and yellow rug, shelves brimming over with books, stuffed toys, and puzzles.

"Here we go," the attendant announced, stopping at an antique roll-up desk. Beside it, fifteen or so albums of old newspapers were displayed in a glass case. She unlocked it.

"This is our premiere collection from the late 1800's. The books are pretty battered from use, but we've tried to protect them the best we can. Not many people study them anymore except maybe a high school student here and there, but it's nice we have them available for someone like yourself who has an interest in the past. Plymouth has a more extensive selection if you don't find what you're looking for here."

Her anxious heart thumped faster than normal. "Thank you. May I use this table?"

"Of course. Donated by Dr. and Mrs. Stricker over twenty-five years ago. If there's anything else I can help you with, just let me know."

"I certainly will. You've been very helpful. Do you have a scanner or copy machine?"

The woman laughed and shook her head. "Scanner, no. Copy machine is right over there. Ten cents per copy and you can pay me. Everyone's on the honor system around here. Helps offset some of our expenses to keep this gem open."

"No problem. I'll let you know when I'm done."

The attendant strutted through the corridors producing creaking boards in her wake.

Her chest rattled from the deep breath. Where in the world should she start? She grabbed the first book on the left side of the cabinet, flying dust caused her nose to tingle. She sneezed.

The first article dated December 31, 1820, recapped headlines from the year. She skimmed through the articles, and if she hadn't been looking for something in particular, could have spent a great deal of time perusing the news of an era that fascinated her.

On January 29th, George IV of the UK ascended the throne on the death at Windsor Castle of his father, George III. In July there was a lengthy article about the revolt under Guglielmo Pepe forcing Ferdinand I of the Two Sicilies to sign a constitution modeled on the Spanish Constitution of 1812.

The article also listed important births throughout the year. Some names she'd never heard before and only recognized Susan B. Anthony and Florence Nightingale. The only death she recognized was King George III and Daniel Boone.

She flipped to the back of the book where it advanced to the late 1850's when an article caught her attention.

CAPTAIN SAMUEL ELDRIDGE EXPANDS
DIVERSE HOLDINGS

It's reported Captain Samuel Eldridge has acquired a majority interest in the following companies over a period of two years, making him one of the most powerful and astute businessmen of this decade, earning him the title of Plymouth's Entrepreneur of the Year. Some holdings include:

Ag Branch, Metropolitan Railroads, Dwight and Lowell Manufacturing Co., Suffolk Insurance Co., Lancaster Lyman and Mills, State Bank and Granite Bank.

In addition to these stock holdings, he is a tea and coffee dealer in Boston. Holdings in these entities nominates him as one of the wealthiest businessmen in the county.

She replaced that book and grabbed one next to it assuming they were in chronological order. Her breath hitched. The first article reported the Eldridge family bought large amounts of acreage, big news in those days. It also appeared on the front cover of the local Boston newspaper.

PROMINENT ELDRIDGE FAMILY PURCHASES LARGE ACREAGE ON CAPE COD BAY

Court records indicate prominent businessman, Captain Samuel Eldridge, has purchased eighty acres of prime land on Cape Cod Bay outside of Plymouth. Records indicate ten acres will be for mowing and tillage and twenty-five for pasture for horses, cows, heifers, and swine. The estate will have an unobstructed half-mile view to the sea, with an eighty-foot bluff overlooking a private quarter mile sandy beach.

According to an exclusive interview with the captain, Boston architects are drawing plans to build a Nineteenth Century, Second Empire, Italianate home. The estimated three-story

three-thousand square foot home will be easily distinguished with its unusual Mansard roof. Barns, sheds, corn cribs, and hennery will be erected on the land as well.

The article was dated October 9, 1861.

She put on her reading glasses for a better view of the next article dated six months later. She quickly skimmed through the short article. The picture captivated her.

The mansion was recognizable with its distinct widow's walk and three chimneys. The image was taken afar and baby saplings had started their growth, making the house appear gargantuan. The property, surrounded by a whitewashed three-rail white picket fence, boasted a horseshoe circular drive, barns and sheds to the side of the mansion.

After she read carefully through the article and attached a yellow sticky note, the next headline caused her to drop her pen.

COMMUNITY LEADER AND ENTREPRENEUR SAMUEL ELDRIDGE'S SON DIES IN TRAGIC ACCIDENT

There was no picture. She skimmed the article which reported Sam Eldridge and his sixteen-year-old son, Kent, had been hunting on the estate. When they returned to the barn to clean rifles, of which Captain Eldridge claimed to have removed the shells, his son's rifle discharged, the bullet hitting him in the face, killing him instantly.

"Oh my, God," she whispered out loud. She tagged the page. The tragedy yanked at her heartstrings, knowing personally how a loss of someone so young was not only devastating to parents but siblings too.

She flipped through several more articles about the village and its growth. The next article stopped her.

ANOTHER TRAGEDY STRIKES THE PROMINENT ELDRIDGE FAMILY

Her eyes fixated to the picture under the article. She recognized the face. It was undeniably the young lady she'd seen in the mansion before the fire. Her body twitched. Why was she suddenly overcome with emotion and excitement?

She composed herself and perused the article slowly, attempting to absorb every word so not to miss a detail.

The prominent Eldridge Family has endured another tragic accident. Their beloved daughter, Belinda Sue, accidentally fell off the bluff in front of their estate on November 2. Details have not been released by the family.

The article was short in comparison to the announcement of the accidental death of his son a year to the day. Rampant thoughts swamped her mind; she couldn't focus on one topic. The reality of the news in print was too much to digest. Captain Eldridge's two children were tragically killed on the estate.

Confused and weary from information overload, she tagged the page and closed the book. She strolled to the counter, still in disbelief of what she'd read.

"Gracious, I thought you were glued to that desk," the lady joked.

The antique nautical clock indicated she'd spent over three hours without moving.

"Is that clock right? I can't believe I've been here that long."

"Everyone is intrigued by the mansion, the Eldridges, and tragic losses. Goes to show all the money in the world can't buy happiness. Sure couldn't in their case, even back in those days. Guess after the death of his children, the captain died a slow and agonizing death back then called paralysis, but most thought he died of a broken heart and grief. Rumored he became paranoid and hid all sorts of collectibles in the house."

"Collectibles?"

"Gossip goes he had one of the rarest coin collections, but who knows what he did with it before he died. Probably dumped it in the ocean and it'll wash ashore like the pipes from the ship that hit the Mary Ann rocks."

She was overwhelmed; her brain needed defragging. How was she to sort out local gossip from fact after reading the articles? There was probably only one person who might be able to shed light on the past and strange happenings in the mansion.

She was going to see him right now.

CHAPTER 25

Samuel Mazalewski rarely got visitors to his humble home on Stage Point. Hidden amongst overgrown sumacs, rosa rigosa, and pesky black locust saplings, the cottage was modest compared to other summer homes, but exactly the way he liked it. His view allowed him to look south over the bay and had private access to the rocky beach below, hidden from tourists.

His two-bedroom bungalow was homey, but had no computers, iPads, Blue-rays, just cable. It was all he needed as long as he had Elly May.

He'd never forget how Elly May, a mellow Jack Russell terrier, became part of his family. Hattie had loved golden retrievers, the sweetest dogs on earth. But, they weren't good with her two horses. After much research, she found Jack Russells, who were bred in England for flushing fox in the hunt, was the type of dog she needed, smallish, quick, and easy to care for.

Hattie dragged him along to see a breeder in Halifax who bred Belgian drafts and Jacks. She loved the runt immediately with its beautiful face, wiggly butt, and white cow spots. He'd never seen a dog cozy up to someone like Elly May did to Hattie the first time.

His philosophy on life was to keep it simple—don't complicate matters. If it's broke, fix it. If it wasn't broke, then why in the hell would anyone want to fix it?

While outspoken and rough around the edges at times, most people adored him, well, at least tolerated him. He made it a point to be there for his friends come hell or high water.

The closest he came to marriage was Hattie, but was afraid it'd change the wonderful, carefree relationship they endured over their lifetimes, each had the space they required. Besides, they both enjoyed a little sin which added some zest to life.

They'd first met at the age of six when they entered first grade, even though both were born in the village. Back then families didn't mingle or get involved with another like they did now, though there was some fence jumping going on amongst kin, second cousins mostly. Some families were related on both sides and if a man married his deceased brother's wife, it could mean real prestige.

The first few years they didn't know the other existed. Attending the small Brook Road School, they were in the same class all the way through eighth grade. He was the cut up of the class and teased her mercilessly. Hattie was quiet and shy. When they aged and matured, they found each other's friendship invaluable and preferred to be together as friends versus romantically.

That all changed when they got older. Their fellowship grew into more. They became secret lovers because Hattie's family was more prominent than his. Her father, while he tolerated Sam, wouldn't acknowledge or allow any romantic involvement. He even went so far as to send her out-of-state to school one year to separate them.

For years they snuck around until they were old enough her father had no say in how Hattie lived her life. They shared many interests, striving to save the earth, sea, and all living creatures. Their mutual causes brought them even closer.

Hattie loved children and animals and, occasionally, they'd discuss marriage. Her father threatened if she married him, the house would be sold. She'd be disinherited. Since the house and land meant everything to her, she lived with the threat.

After her mother passed away from cancer when Hattie was fifteen, she cared for her father in the mansion until he passed at age sixty-two from emphysema and chronic kidney disease.

Finally free to join lives as man and wife, he and Hattie were old enough they didn't want children at the age of forty. They were content with their lives and okay with the reality that their love would not be shared with bands. He loved and missed that woman. She was one of a kind.

The gentle rap on the door caused him to struggle to get out of his worn brown recliner. Elly May was sound asleep next to him and didn't budge. She'd lost her hearing years ago, but was in pretty good form for ninety dog years. While deafness was a handicap, she sensed anything around and not much got by her. Her daily activities of running up and down the beach bluff and stairs kept her in trim shape. Too bad it didn't work that way for him.

"Well, hi there, sweet pea. Come on in. How ya doing?"

The creaking screen door swung open and allowed Kelli to pass through; her perfume lingered gardenias.

She embraced him tightly, causing his shoulders to ache, which they did daily from RA and rotator cuff surgery five years ago. The doctor told him he needed to quit hauling lobster pots, but did he listen?

"Sorry I've dropped by unannounced. Hope it's okay?"

"Are ya kiddin' me, sweetie. I don't get many visitors, especially from pretty young ladies like ya. Come on in and have a seat. Can I get ya something to drink? 'Bout all I've got these days is some Sam Adams and maybe a Coca Coklie." He mispronounced Cola for her benefit. He always loved to tease her.

She laughed. He loved that girl, her laugh and sense of humor. So opposite of him, the grumpy ole' man, on the outside, at least.

"Sure, Coke sounds great. Could use a little caffeine buzz about now."

"Comin' right up." He made his way into a kitchen about the size of a large closet and retrieved a can of Coke from the old rounded refrigerator not much taller than him. "So, what brings ya my way? Can't remember the last time ya came down here. Ya were always at Hattie's house."

"Maz, I don't know where to start to be honest. Since I've been in town, so many things have happened. Did you hear there was a fire at the mansion yesterday?"

"Yepper, everybody yapped 'bout it at the restaurant this mornin'. Said ya were home but weren't hurt and wasn't much damage done. Thank God for both."

"I think someone's trying to hurt or scare me. This is the second incident since I came back. That's too many as far as I'm concerned. Police aren't taking any of this seriously. They blame it on loose plaster in the house, kids playing with matches. I don't buy it. Something isn't right. I feel it in my gut."

He sat next to her on the worn brown fabric couch, sagging by his weight. He placed his rough weathered hand on top of hers.

"Honey, go with yar instincts. Hattie had an in-tune intuition. Maybe ya've inherited that. She constantly got weird feelings and most of the time she was right on the money. She'd never say she was a psychic, but I swear she was at times."

"One of the reasons I stopped by was to ask you about the mansion. You know that property inside and out, probably almost as well as Hattie since you spent so much time there."

"That I did. Best times of my life." He scratched his scruffy beard which hadn't been trimmed in months.

"Well, I went to the library today and got articles about the mansion and the Eldridge family. I thought of anyone in town, you'd help me sort out what is fact or fiction."

"Sweetie, I'd do anything in the world to help ya and ya know that. My memory isn't what it used to be, but I'd give it a whirl."

Elly May readjusted herself in the recliner when she realized the warm body was gone and relocated next to him on the couch. When he had gotten out of the hospital from his bypass back in the day, Hattie waited on him hand and foot. When she was away, Elly May took on the responsibility and over time became his constant companion. Even though she was Hattie's dog, nobody told Elly May.

"Gracious, I don't even know where to start. I know you'll be totally honest with me. Hattie believed in Belinda's ghost, didn't she?"

"Yep," he answered without hesitation. "I swear I've seen her too on the widow's walk on full moons. A few times when we came back from the bluff, we'd see her. Hattie had numerous encounters in the house where she'd show up, occasionally hide or move things."

"I don't know if it's because I'm stressed, but I swear, and don't laugh at me, an entity spoke to me yesterday. Said I was in danger. Do you have any idea what all of this could mean? Throw on top of that the strange accidents in the house, it has started to scare the shit out of me."

He drew in a deep breath which caused his chest to rise and fall, a common occurrence when concerned. His lungs were in poor shape from smoking all those years; he hacked raspingly.

"Gracious, ya do have a lot of questions," he joked, trying to make light before he answered seriously. "Kelli, only ya know what ya saw and heard. I can't validate that for ya. Wish Hattie was here to help ya through this, but if she was, ya wouldn't be dealing with any of this, would ya? Go with your intuition.

"From all the research Hattie had done and rumors from generations handed down, she was one-hundred percent convinced Eldridge stole treasures from the *Forest Queen*.

"If my memory recalls correctly, in the mid-1800's a violent storm created a rogue wave, and the *Forest Queen* confused the lighthouses at Scituate for Minot Light and ran ashore near Pegotty Beach.

"Story went twelve tons of silver ingots cast in China were on board when she sank, which no one knew about. She was a cargo ship and was supposed to carry cargo, but not that kind. Eldridge somehow recovered the treasure and hid it in the mansion or on his property.

"Hattie occasionally found an ingot someplace so conspicuous it was silly. Times she'd cleaned and turned around, and there one was."

"Seriously? All those years, she never said a word to me about that. But, that's exactly what happened to me. One minute it wasn't there, the next it was. How does one explain that?"

"Hattie figured it was Belinda. Signs to hang on to the house. The silver enabled Hattie to do that. I doubt she confided in anyone other than me, but when she went to Boston, one ingot bar fetched close to five thousand dollars."

"Wow. That's unbelievable."

He toyed with his beard. "That's how Hattie kept the mansion's repairs up. When things got rough around the edges, one of these ingots showed up. She even had a few occasions where a rare coin appeared on the mantel in the main parlor or an antique bell on the grand staircase.

"Wish I could remember more about the coins. Think she kept a log somewhere about what she cashed in and their values. If I recollect right, want to say she found a gold five dollar half eagle and a dollar with some weird name like Gobrecht or something like that."

Kelli's face reflected disbelief. He'd been shocked too when Hattie shared this secret only with him.

"Signs from a ghost? Is that what Hattie thought? Was this about the time they figured she had early signs of Alzheimer's?" she asked.

"Yepper, sure was. Before she got that damn crooked disease, I was the only one she told about her sightings and findings. But when her brain started slowly being destroyed, she'd talk all the time with Belinda Eldridge."

"This is all so unbelievable. I mean I believe you, but it's all so strange."

"When she'd talk about coins in the house, they knew she'd lost her mind. Guess Bubba Smithe's sister helped out in the nursing home and divulged things Hattie said to Bubba, which should have never happened. What happened to confidentiality?

"But between you and me, sweetie, I think she was dead on serious about everything she said, even though at times she was looney as a tune, bless her sweet soul."

"But you believed her, didn't you? Before and after she got sick?"

"I always understood her, but when the illness progressed, sometimes her stories didn't make sense. She'd repeat the same thing over and over. But what's happening to ya, Kelli, I don't know what advice to give. She always said, don't give into fear, give into your instincts. That's probably the best advice I'd offer ya or anyone else."

He drew her close and wrapped his weary arms around her pint-sized frame. She was the closest thing to a daughter he'd ever have and was closer to her than his bratty wealthy niece out west who never gave him the time of day.

"Captain Maz, thanks. I knew you'd be the one person I could confide in without feeling stupid and you'd take me seriously. I don't know what's happening in that house. I don't know why someone obviously wants me out of there. But guess what? It's not going to happen. If there's one thing Auntie taught me, it was to stand my ground. That's exactly what I intend to do."

CHAPTER 26

Kelli convinced herself after her conversation with Captain Maz she could face whatever waited for her at the mansion. If someone had tried to scare her away, they hadn't succeeded. She wasn't budging.

If it hadn't been for her strong will and love for Auntie, she would've taken Rod's offer and been out of town by now, vacationing on some tropical beach with a cocktail garnished with fresh fruit.

No. She wasn't running—this time. When Steve died, she'd put her head in the sand and didn't deal with the situation the way she should have. She rationalized, made every excuse why he hadn't confided in her, which brought her to an all-time low in her self-esteem.

When she pulled in the lane, the house looked eerily barren. While curious, she didn't want to face the damage the small fire had done. Perhaps it'd been teenagers smoking weed or cigarettes and was an accident. The area was in a severe drought and everything was dry and brittle, including wood piled in the backyard with dead ragweed, milkweed, and golden rod laid on top.

A southeast wind picked up. The radio announced a nasty thunderstorm with hail and high winds was headed their way. That was all she needed tonight, a weather disturbance after she jumped through hoops to get her electricity restored. She had to battle with the power company to reinstate the service since the wiring was dangerously out of code. They allowed her service for thirty days and after that it had to be updated or it would be shut off permanently. From the culmination of events, she was ill at ease to stay in the house alone, but too proud to ask for help.

She ascended the winding staircase to the bedroom and bounced when she settled on the airbed. Nothing had been moved. Rancidity of smoke permeated throughout.

Why are these things happening to me? What have I ever done but help people and do what was right, and now all this? My life is out of control and I can't see a clear way out. I pray for strength and understanding.

A thundering clap of lightning caused her to tumble the short distance to the floor. She was close to exhaustion, her nerves shot. All she wanted was to lie down and close her weary eyes. Lack of sleep had taken a toll on every part of her body, especially her eyes, since she suffered from dry eye syndrome.

She nestled on the bed and wrapped her fleecy blanket around her legs even though it was warm. Dampness from the steady stream of rain chilled her, and the downpour picked up in intensity. The cracked window next to the bed allowed in a dewy reserve.

It wasn't long before the breeze, mist, and patter of raindrops on the old shingles relaxed her. While she slowly drifted off, her flight of fancy placed her in a different era. It was like a motion picture where characters played their roles to perfection.

The mansion, in all its magnificence and pristine condition, was the backdrop. She sat in the grass in the front yard under the old Gingko tree. The mansion was painted beige, not a board or shingle loose, lawn and shrubs manicured.

A horse-drawn carriage pulled up to the front of the house in the circular drive. From within the house a preteen skinny girl in braided pigtails ran out. She didn't recognize the child at first, but she was familiar. The girl climbed in the carriage, and she and a man were whisked away by a well-matched pair of horses.

A young boy ran out of the house and down the lane to catch them. Dust swallowed him up. A short, staunchy woman appeared on the porch with a long dress and apron and waved while the carriage made its way to the gravel road past the white picket fence. The boy didn't catch them, so he slowly treaded back to the porch where the woman wrapped her arm around his shoulder, and they entered the house.

The mansion's décor was rich, eclectic, and ornate and overflowed with excessive decorations. Embellished fabrics and furnishings were lavish in jewel tones with deep reds, emerald and forest greens, gold, and browns. Divans were dotted with needlepoint pillows, fresh wisteria flopped over the decorative vase, potted palms in corners.

The place reeked of wealth and prominence, from its dark wood moldings and cornices to patterned floral designed wallpapers and hand-crafted furniture. Oriental area rugs adorned each room. The round large dining table with hand carved legs and marble slab sat on a jumbo rug.

Extensive paintings and a family photograph of four plus the family Lab were proudly displayed in embellished gold frames. Antique china was displayed in the corner built-in dining room cabinet; the serving pantry was full of utensils and dishes. In the kitchen several servants giggled while they banged pots and pans. Ham and turkey aromas drifted into the room.

She glided to the second floor into a beautiful bedroom. It must have belonged to the girl she just saw. The oversized feather bed had a carved canopy in pink and white hues and blended perfectly with the matching damask wall covering. Beautiful dolls filled the heavy armoire, ornately carved with an artistic washbowl on a washstand.

She floated down the hall into a bathroom where a lady scrubbed a gilded claw-foot tub. It was hard to distinguish whether she was Indian or African American.

A noise within the house startled her awake. She sat up, disoriented from the dream. Was someone downstairs? The storm had moved in with a vengeance. A clap of thunder in close proximity reverberated in the room. Loose panes of glass rattled. It was dark. How long had she slept? The clatter downstairs intensified. Was someone rummaging through the house?

"They are here to harm you," a meek voice announced.

No one was in the bedroom. Where did the voice come from?

"What? Who is it?" she asked, her heart racing.

"Beware."

A loud thud came from the upstairs hallway outside the bedroom. She shivered and broke out in a cold sweat. Through the darkness an explosion blended hues of colors when it penetrated the room. Her eardrums pounded from the heavy pressure. It was seconds before the loud pop filled the room. Had a firework gone off beside her?

Then glass shattered behind her head; shards splattered her and the room with pin-like needles. She clutched both ears to stop the bullet blast from piercing her eardrums which reverberated inside her head. Even though her ears pulsed and were covered, a loud commotion bellowed from the staircase.

Shocked and confused, she unsteadily made her way to the doorway. Splinters of glass pierced her bare feet. She glanced over the banister to the curved stairs and entryway. Someone wearing a hoody ran out the front door.

Woozy, bewildered, and light-headed, she scooted on the floor until her back was flat against the flaking wallpaper in the hall which caught on her tee shirt. She gasped and tried to take one breath at a time, until she stopped shaking. Her ears throbbed.

Am I losing my mind? Someone just tried to kill me.

CHAPTER 27

The storm that blew through Manomet was violent and knocked out power to Rod's motor coach. He flipped on the generator which gave him all the conveniences of home.

Worried about Kelli, he fidgeted and paced. Had the mansion lost power too? Was Kelli by herself in the dark? Why should he be concerned? She wasn't his responsibility, but he cared about her well-being—and maybe more.

Instead of fretting all night, he grabbed a yellow poncho and dashed to his truck in the pelting rain. The wind and claps of thunder subsided slightly, then renewed its intensity and came down sideways. Overhead branches hung heavy, nearly touching the pavement and leaves littered the two-lane road which caused him to swerve. When he reached the old mansion, large limbs crisscrossed the drive and made it impossible to get up the lane. He parked in the wet yard and grabbed a flashlight out of the glove compartment. He sprinted to the porch where one of the double doors stood open.

"Kelli," he yelled, poking his head in while rain and wind swirled. "Are you here?" he called louder.

"Up here," a distressed voice answered.

He mounted two stairs at a time up the long staircase. The beam spotted her sitting in the dark hallway. He kneeled. His knee caught a loose board with an exposed nail which ripped his pants and flesh.

"Are you okay? What happened?"

"I...I don't know," she whimpered. "Someone tried to...kill me."

"What?"

"Someone shot at me in the bedroom." Her hands covered her ears; her body shuddered.

"Let's not jump to conclusions."

"Look in there. I know what happened. You weren't here. I was," she exclaimed.

"You're right. Slowly tell me what happened."

"I was sleeping and woke when I heard noises downstairs. Before I knew, there was an explosion in my bedroom. Someone shot at me and hit the window. Glass is everywhere. Go see for yourself. Someone tried to kill me," she wailed.

Unknowingly, he had placed his hand on her ice cold knee. It twitched uncontrollably. She was visibly distraught. He surveyed the bedroom with his flashlight; glass fragments sparkled in the ray. One panel of the brittle window was shattered with jagged shards of glass exposed around the frame.

Maybe someone shot at her to scare her? Would this mean the other occurrences weren't an accident or coincidence after all?

Weeping echoed from the hall. When he returned, Kelli's head was propped on her knees.

"Hey, I'm really sorry this happened to you." He positioned his arm around her trembling shoulder and drew her close.

"I don't think I can go on like this. Maybe I should sell. Maybe I should get out of town. I should listen to Belinda."

"Belinda? Who's Belinda?"

"She's the ghost who lives here."

She's hit the wall. She talks to ghosts?

"Kelli, I think it'd be a good idea if you got out of here. Why don't we go back to my boat where you can get cleaned up and rest. You won't be alone there."

"I don't know what to do. I don't want to impose."

"No imposition. Here, let me help you up. Do you need to grab anything?"

Her legs wobbled. Obviously, she was physically drained from the experience. Maybe it was the accumulation of what she'd gone through. She borrowed his flashlight and tossed a few items in a small travel bag and joined him in the hall.

She walked down the staircase and held tightly onto the banister as she took each step. He followed closely. Maybe he should be in front in case she tumbled.

"Is there anything else you need to do before we leave?"

"Just lock the front door. That's all. Here's the key."

He bolted the door, pulled on the handle twice to make sure it was secure. The rain and wind returned; swirls of pellets whipped against their bodies. He helped her into the truck. Her unsteady legs shook harder.

He backed up the truck and pulled onto the long gravel driveway. The wind whipped the vehicle with leaves. "Kelli, relax for a minute. I'm going to call the police."

"I can't go through another interrogation right now. Can we report this tomorrow?"

"Let me call it in and we're on our way to the boat where you'll be safe. They're too many things going on that aren't adding up."

She slumped into the side of the cab and rested her head on the fogged window.

"What's your emergency?" a lady on the other end of the phone asked.

"This is Rod Kesson. I'm calling on behalf of Kelli Goddard who lives in the Manomet Mansion. Someone just shot a bullet into the window which barely missed her. We're at the mansion now. Can you immediately send over an officer?"

"Is Ms. Goddard hurt? Do we need an ambulance?"

"She is quite shaken, but no ambulance. Can you send someone now? I want to get her out of here."

"Yes, sir. I've dispatched an officer. He's over at Stowell's Café across the street eating dinner and should be there momentarily."

"Thank you."

Kelli had closed her eyes; moisture accumulated on her cheeks.

"Can I get you anything? Here, throw this jacket on. Maybe you'll stop shivering." He pulled the jacket from the back seat and stroked her shoulder while he covered her.

"All I want right now is to get out of here. I don't understand why these things are happening. You don't know anything about this, do you?" She looked at him pleadingly.

He was stunned and taken aback by her question. "How would I know anything about this?"

"How convenient you would show up when you did. You're the only person I know that has an interest in this old house, other than me."

"Interest, yes. And you think I would go to these tactics to get possession of it? You're dead wrong, Kelli. Thanks for the vote of confidence."

"I'm sorry. I'm so confused."

The wail of the siren from the police cruiser stopped their conversation. He leaped out of the truck and ran to the side of the squad car that came to a quick halt, trying to shield himself from the rain and wind.

Gregg Scott rolled down his window. "What's going on here? Is Kelli okay?"

"Yes, she's fine. Shaken a bit. Someone fired a shot into the upstairs bedroom where she was sleeping. She heard someone come up the stairs, but didn't actually see who it was."

"Well, I need to get the facts from her," Officer Scott replied with an attitude. He made his way to the side of the truck where Kelli sat. He opened the door. "Kelli, you all right?"

"Yes." Her voice wavered. "Why is someone doing this?"

"I don't know, but I guarantee I'll get to the bottom of it. Is the house unlocked?"

"No. We locked it up, but there's an extra key on top of the double doors. Let yourself in and lock up when you're done."

"Gotcha. Do you want to get in the cruiser and I'll take you to the Blue Spruce? I don't think we're going to have power until tomorrow when this storm is over."

"That's not necessary. Kelli's coming with me," Rod interjected. I have more than enough space on the yacht for her to rest comfortably, plus I can ensure no one will bother her there."

Gregg looked at Kelli. "Is that what you want to do?"

"Right now, I really don't care where I go. I just need to get away from here."

He darted to her side of the truck and wedged himself between her and the officer and shut the door gently. Kelli slumped against the window.

"Here's my card. Give me a call after you look over the situation and let me know what you find. Put your best men on this, would you? I'd appreciate it."

"I bet you would," Gregg replied nastily.

Once in the truck, he pulled forward to avoid the downed limbs, so he could make his way to Brewers Boat Yard. It was a quiet drive although he dodged limbs and debris. He occasionally glanced at Kelli. Since her eyes were closed, he didn't engage her in conversation. The best thing he could do for her right now would be to get her someplace where she felt safe and secure. He could promise her that on the yacht.

His mind contemplated different scenarios. Why were these things happening to her? Sure appeared the accidents were intended to hurt Kelli or scare her away. And she was correct in that he was the only person she could think of that had a vested interest in the mansion.

He parked in his reserved spot at the marina. Bringing Kelli there under these circumstances was the last thing he envisioned doing. He cast a brief glance at her. She sat upright and ran her fingers through her damp hair.

"Rod, I don't know if this is a good idea. I really could stay at the Blue Spruce."

"Sure you could. But on the yacht, I can assure you total rest, security, and electricity. Doubt the Blue Spruce or anyone in town has power from what I saw driving here."

"I don't want to be a bother."

"No prob. Hey, there's no inconvenience. I have more than enough space. You'll have your own suite and total privacy."

He slid out quickly to make sure she wouldn't change her mind. With one hand on her elbow, he unlocked the gate with the security card. They briskly walked down the dark boardwalk. Even though the rain had stopped, the wind churned. A towering, thickset man in a black trench coat stood by the boat to assist while they climbed aboard.

"Thanks, Guy," he acknowledged. "You okay, Kelli?"

She appeared sheepishly white when he offered his hand to assist her up the stairs.

"Yeah, just not feeling great. Hate to be a party pooper, but I really need to lie down."

"I totally understand. Let me show you to your quarters."

He grabbed her chilled hand and strolled into the combined living and dining area. He'd handpicked each item in the yacht from the neutral colored carpet and leather chairs to the excessive recessed lighting with dimmers in the shiny ceiling. Even though a yacht, he wanted the interior to portray warmth and comfort.

Nautical collections from his scuba days were displayed on the tables, his parents' picture a backdrop. A beige throw and yellow roses in a teal vase boasted tasteful accents.

Spiral stairs led below deck. He designed to impress, and it was opulent even by his standards. Everything was varnished and shiny, there wasn't a handprint anywhere. They passed the gym and movie theater before they reached the first guest suite.

He threw open the two-by-two wooden varnished doors. The guest quarters had been designed to be almost as plethoric as his master suite, this one themed in animal prints with lavish mink rug and throw.

"Oh, my God. I've never seen anything like this except in magazines. Most homes aren't this extravagant."

"Thanks. It's mostly to impress business associates and possible investors."

"Well, I'm neither, but thanks for letting me stay. I really don't want to be alone tonight. I apologize for the snide remark earlier. That was uncalled for. I'm under a lot of pressure, if you can't tell."

"Snide remark?"

"Yeah, the one about you possibly being involved in what's happened to me and the house." She shivered from the air conditioning while she strolled around the suite.

"I didn't take it personal, Kelli. You've been through a lot. This would unnerve anyone. Apology accepted. I believe you'll find what you need. Robe and slippers behind the door and necessary toiletries in the bathroom. Perhaps a nice salt lavender bath in the sunken Jacuzzi with champagne might relax you."

She nervously snickered. "You sound like a host on the travel channel. I assume you entertain ladies quite often on this magnificent home on the sea."

"Travel channel guide? No way. Ladies...there's been a few, but we're not going there. You should rest. If you need anything, dial zero and the butler will bring whatever you desire. There's an assortment of beverages in your refrigerator, along with fresh fruit and veggies. Just let him know what you want."

"Gracious, you've thought of everything, haven't you?"

"I try."

"Rod. Thanks. I sincerely appreciate it and apologize for my attitude. There was no call for that."

"It's okay. And so you have peace of mind, we're going to troll the waters slowly, so you'll be one-hundred percent safe on this boat. You might even find the slight movement soothing."

"Been on boats all my life and the way I feel right now, a couple glasses of champagne and I'll be out like a light...I hope. God knows I need the rest. Good night and thanks again."

"Night. Hope you sleep well."

He returned to the back of the boat where he called the captain and instructed him to slowly cruise Cape Cod Bay, far enough from shore not to be disturbed. Thankfully, the rain and wind had subsided.

He kicked off his soaked loafers and found his favorite blue and white lounger on the open-air sundeck next to the hot tub that allowed a view without getting wet.

He sat a few minutes before the butler arrived with his favorite vodka drink with blue cheese olives and a plate of deviled eggs, his favorite recipe from his mother.

He propped his feet on the lounger, lit a cigar, and blew smoke in circles above his head. Rain dripped from the canopy. What a day for this poor woman...what a five years.

Why do I feel so protective? Because she's vulnerable? Alone and needs someone? Or am I the lonely one?

Her natural style appealed to him. He'd never dated anyone like her, nor would he probably get the chance with her walls up. She was honest, trustworthy, self-sufficient, while compassionate. He wanted to hold her, to make her world okay. She so deserved that after all she'd been through.

He considered himself a loving and caring person. Over the years, he attempted to live up to his father's expectations which influenced him to be ruthless and non-caring to get the job done. His father's intentions were to let the dollar dictate how he treated people, but thankfully his mother kept him grounded with unwavering love and concern.

This woman had guts, that was for sure. By now most ladies would've taken the money or even one-third and ran. She had fortitude, principles, beliefs she wasn't willing to waive. He respected that. There was so much more he wanted to know. He was unsure if it was because he hadn't been in a serious relationship for several years, but he had an undeniable attraction to her.

The boat lazily glided through the sea; waves splashed against the hull. After another couple of drinks, he downed the remaining deviled eggs and stretched out. The storm had passed leaving a crescent moon, star dotted sky, and a temperature ten degrees cooler.

He loved the outdoors regardless of weather, but his preference was warmth to cold. Trips out west to his parents' home in Lake Tahoe were enjoyable. It was cozy around a roaring, crackling fire in the two-story stone fireplace, snow drifts covering the ground and evergreens.

If he had his druthers, he'd be on a boat and the more tropical setting the better; sand between his toes, cocktails with umbrellas and fruit, jet skis at his disposal. A hottie in a skimpily clad bikini on his arm would top off the setting.

"Boss."

He flinched, his thoughts suspended. "Yes?"

"Think you need to check on your guest. I was getting your room ready and heard her crying and throwing up. Thought you should be aware."

He glided his hand over his day old beard and down his throat. "Not sure what to do, Sy. This lady's had her share of troubles."

"Just wanted to alert you," Sy added and left the deck. The man had been with him for fifteen years.

He recognized what his tone indicated.

Okay, this is a fine line. Do I let her be, so she can let out her emotions or should I see if I can help? Against his better judgment, he got up and made his way to her suite.

He positioned himself outside the door for a few minutes. Uncontrollable sobbing echoed into the hall. He almost chickened out and went back upstairs, but he should at least try to help. He couldn't stand to see a woman cry, for any reason, especially if he was the cause.

He tapped on the door. The crying slowed. He tapped again.

"Kelli, you all right?"

No response. Then the door gradually opened. Her eyes were reddish and cheeks dewy. A plush white robe swathed her body.

"You okay?"

"Guess I had to let out all these pent up emotions and got a little seasick. Sorry if I bothered you." She sniffed.

"You didn't bother me. Sy heard you and was concerned. Can we get you anything?"

"No, I'll be fine. Maybe a couple of aspirins. I have a terrible headache and my ears are pounding."

While he stood in the entry to her suite, the boat rocked severely to one side, causing her to fall into his arms, tossing both into the suite. The double doors slammed.

As a natural reaction, he grabbed her, held her close to his chest. The warmth of her body penetrated through the plush robe.

Her arms tugged him closer and held tightly. He gazed into her watery eyes which allowed him into the portal of her soul. Naturally, he angled his face and focused on her pink, moist swollen lips.

He softly indicated his voracious invitation. She accepted. Slowly, passionately, he captured her mouth with hungry urgency. His tongue caressed her salty lips and danced with hers. Their bodies entangled.

She pulled away. "I'm sorry, Rod. That shouldn't have happened." She turned her back and stroked her cheek. "I'm not ready for this. My emotions are out of control. It's been a long day. Let's say goodnight, okay?"

"Hmmm…thought you were enjoying it too." His body quivered from withdrawal from her warmth.

"Can we just call it a night?"

"No problem." He backed out of the suite and closed the doors. He leaned against the slick wall, confused but yearned to go back and hold her. Protect her. He wanted more.

Did she just reject me? No. His heart and physical indications told him differently. He darted to the balcony.

Sy appeared. "Sorry, Boss. Captain said there was a small boat without lights, and he had to swerve to miss it. Stupid idiot."

Small boat out in the middle of Cape Cod Bay with no lights on a night like this? That was odd. Something wasn't right.

CHAPTER 28

Without much consideration, Rod returned to the guest suite and rapped on the door. Kelli answered. Still wrapped in the fluffy white robe, one bare shoulder was exposed while she held it closed at the waist.

"I'm sorry to bother you, but the captain said there was a boat without lights that almost hit us. That's why the yacht shifted so quickly. That's highly unusual for this area since it's patrolled heavily by the Harbor Master. That'd be a hefty fine to be out at night without your running lights on.

"I don't want to alarm you, but we need to be cautious. We're both too drained. I think it might be best if I slept on the couch over there. I'll feel better if I'm close in case of an emergency. And I'm not saying this because of what just happened between us. It's purely from a safety standpoint. Honest."

She turned her back to him. His imagination stirred. What was under the robe she wore? He rotated her around.

He stared into her eyes while he held her shoulders. "I promise. Nothing will happen between us. Scout's honor," he teased and made the sign.

"Can I hold you to that?"

"You bet."

"Okay. Guess you know where the sheets and blankets are since this is your boat. But do you really think this is necessary? What harm could a small boat be to a yacht this size?"

"I don't want to scare you, but the Kesson's wealth makes us a target for kidnappers, ransom, and—"

"And what?"

"With all that's been going on, we can't take any chances if someone is after you."

"Great. Just great," she complained.

He opened the cabinets below the fifty-inch flat screen and threw out beige sheets, a fluffy blanket, and pillow onto the oversized leather couch.

"Everything will be fine. No need to worry. The crew upstairs will watch round the clock. They're fully trained for these types of situations. One of the guys in my crew is a former CIA agent." He struggled to make his bed.

He sensed she was nervous by the way her legs fidgeted as she sat on the edge of the bed. She crossed and uncrossed her arms, pulling tight the robe around her chest.

He pretended not to gaze while she slid into the bed. She fumbled under the comforter and when she threw out the robe her panties and a sheer halter were exposed. Her nearly-naked body glided onto the satin sheets. He was aroused knowing how silky that felt on her skin.

"Lights out?" he asked.

"Sure…but can you leave on the one in the bathroom and the door cracked? My stomach is still unsettled."

"No prob."

The lights were out, but there was an aura that arched invisibly between them. How could she fall asleep so quickly? He sure as hell had trouble thinking about anything except for the woman in the same room with him. Had she taken a sleeping pill?

He tossed and turned for hours. A soft whimpering flowed from the other side of the room.

"Kelli, you okay?" he whispered.

She didn't answer.

Shit—do I check on her or will she think I'm trying to make advances.

"Kelli?"

No answer.

He threw off the blanket and tip-toed to the side of her bed, forgetting he only had on Nike boxers. He stood over her. She tossed, turned, and wept in her sleep. Not sure what to do, he sat on the edge of the bed and hoped she'd wake from whatever turmoil haunted her.

She screamed.

Shit. He fell to the floor. Without consideration and on his knees, he touched her shoulder. "Kelli, wake up. You've had a bad dream."

She flung to both sides, finally curling to face him. When her eyes opened, she gasped.

"It's okay. You must have had a nightmare. You screamed. Just checking to make sure you're okay. Nothing more."

"I'm sorry. I have repetitious dreams of my husband's car accident, only it's me instead of him and I'm drowning." She laid back on the pillow; her bare arm covered her dewy eyes.

"Would you like me to stay close to you? I promise I won't try anything." He positioned himself on the edge of the bed.

She hesitated briefly then snuggled next to him. She picked up the sheet. "Yes. But you have to stay on your side of the bed. Promise?"

"Deal." His body slid between the silky sheets, an arm's length distance from her.

She turned on her side, leaving him staring at her back. He attempted to get more comfortable, rearranged the pillow, and threw off the blanket. Had lying next to her made him hotter than normal? He couldn't sleep like a mummy all night since he always slept on his side.

The silence was unnatural. He shut his eyes and attempted to forget the sensuous woman next to him. The stimulating connection was undeniable, even though their bare skins weren't touching.

The yacht swayed sharply again. This time she slid into him and both almost fell off the bed. He regrouped and returned to his warm spot, but she didn't move.

"What was that?"

"Not sure. Sailing at night can sometimes be dangerous in these waters. Maybe they had to avoid a whale or rock. Who knows? Don't concern yourself. If there's anything I need to know, the captain will call."

"So, the captain knows we're...sleeping together?" she asked, concern in her voice.

"The captain knows I'm sleeping on the couch for your protection."

"Protection? From you or pirates?"

"This is only for your safety and no other reason." Was he grumpy because his testosterone level had peaked because an attractive, single, nearly naked woman lay next to him?

"I'm grateful, Rod. I really am. Can I ask a favor and not have you judge me?"

"Sure, just don't ask me to crawl out of this cozy bed."

"Could we cuddle?"

Cuddle? When has anyone ever asked me to cuddle other than his mother?

"What's your definition of cuddling?" he joked to break up the tense moment.

"I want someone to hold me, show me I'm not alone in this world, especially with all that's gone on. Having a warm body in bed is probably the thing I've missed the most since my husband...died. I detest sleeping alone."

Her explanation shocked him. It indicated vulnerability and, more importantly, willingness to admit it. She was the most candid woman he'd ever met, definitely not a gamer.

"Well, can't say I'm a great snuggler, but I can hold you. I assure you I'll do everything in my power to protect you tonight."

She awkwardly slid closer, lying on her side. She braced her body with one arm to face him and pulled up the sheet over her chest.

He moved to his side and gazed at her, even more aware of the physical effect she had on him. He scooted closer where their bare bodies touched, warmth circulated around them. His muscled left arm wrapped around her slender body, fingers caressed her back. Her body relaxed.

"I can't tell you how great that feels. I've missed that human touch." She sighed.

"Feels dandy to me too." He attempted a joke while his hand glided up and down her spine which occasionally caught the top of her bikini brief. Her body released against his. There wasn't enough light to distinguish if her eyes were open or closed.

His pulse accelerated. How could he sleep all night like this without more? He wanted to make love to her worse than any woman he'd ever been with.

Without warning, her arm drew him closer. Her aroused peaks touched his bare chest. He squirmed.

Her finger traced his nipple. He fought for a breath, his inner groin ablaze.

What in the hell is she doing to me?

With pressure on his chest, she moved into position. Her steamy lips sent an invitation.

Urgent to reciprocate, he questioned, "Kelli, do you know the effect you're having on me?"

"Absolutely," she whispered in his ear.

"You sure you want to go there?"

"Positive. I need someone to make love to me again, show me I'm worthy. If you don't want to, well, that's—"

He put his finger to her velvety lips and stopped the conversation. He rolled her so her back was against the mattress. Now he was in control. Her body shuddered under the weight of his leg that crossed over hers. Bare skin glided in unison.

He captured her mouth with hungry urgency; his tongue darted repeatedly inside. He tenderly kneaded and stroked her honey soft breasts, one at a time. He slid his hand to her navel, stopped only to caress it, then on to the door of her femininity, damp with anticipation.

He leisurely slipped on top of her smooth, hot frame. Intoxicated by her slow, calculated movements, he caressed her arms, merged their hands, and interlaced their fingers. Knowing their bodies screamed for more, he penetrated with slow, wanting motion and rotation, his tool iron-hard.

She responded with quick jerks. Her legs writhed. She released agonized gasps.

Each thrust was independent and soothing, and he took his time to savor every second of their intimate lovemaking. Her kisses were explicit come-and-get-me. He captured her lips again.

She surprised him with a roll and landed him on his back, their union still intact. She was in control now. She sat upright which exposed her firm breasts, nipples dimpled and protruded.

He was at her mercy. His heart raced so quickly, he didn't care if he died of a heart attack at that moment. He'd die the happiest man on earth.

Her hands caressed his muscled flesh. When she leaned to kiss his throbbing lips, her soft, ripe swollen nipples stroked his chest.

She returned to a sitting position, his engorged manhood at stiff attention. They moved in unison to her physical demands. He thrusted deeper, her accepting all he could give. The pace quickened. She writhed against his thighs, her rhythm desperate.

Not able to take another moment, he quickened his thrusts. He sucked in air while spasms of delight rocketed through him. Her breath was shallow and pants fast.

Loud, ecstatic groans in union escaped. They shuddered in breaths of gasping completion. She collapsed on his chest. His mouth covered hers while he absorbed her drugging nectar.

"You're a wonderful lover," he whispered.

"Bet you say that to all the girls," she teased with little breaths.

"Never. That was incredible."

She readjusted herself and turned on her side. "I have trouble believing that. Let's face it. We come from totally different backgrounds. You could have any woman you want. You're attractive, wealthy. Not bad in bed."

"But I only want you."

"Why?"

"That's a dumb question. I hoped you felt the same way. Words can't describe the connection we have. Don't you sense it too?"

"Well, yes, but I'm afraid to admit it. I'm afraid to care again."

"It's never too late to love again." He pulled her into his chest and held her tightly.

CHAPTER 29

"Officer Scott, please," Rod commanded from his phone, impatience in his voice.

"What can I do for you, Mr. Kesson?" Gregg answered gruffly. He shuffled the manila folders on his unorganized desk.

"Checking to see what you found out about the shot fired last night at the mansion."

"First, Mr. Kesson, this is a police matter. It's against policy to divulge investigation results to anyone other than those involved. You weren't involved, were you?"

"How would I be?"

"You're the only person I can think of that has an interest in that property, possibly to the extent of wanting to harm Kelli, or scare her away."

"That's ludicrous and you know it. Why don't you get your ass in gear and get serious about finding out what's going on. If need be, I'll bring in my own team of investigators if you locals can't get the job done."

"Whoa, Kesson. Our department's the finest in the state, and how dare you insinuate we aren't doing our job properly? I take personal offense to not only you demeaning my department, but the fact you've shoved yourself in Kelli Goddard's face. Kelli's a lifelong friend of mine. I don't like anything about your intentions."

"My intentions are to help a woman in need and that's exactly what she is right now, so I suggest you focus on police matters. I'll focus on Kelli."

"Yeah, bet you will. Stay out of the way, Kesson. That's all I'm saying."

"I'll expect a thorough report by the end of the week. Kelli's not going to stay in that house alone until we know what happened and those responsible are apprehended."

The phone clicked in his ear. He was pissed at the condescending attitude of this man. Just because Kesson had money and status didn't give him the right to look down on him or his department. Rod Kesson obviously had something going on with Kelli, or he wouldn't be so obstinate with his attitude.

He couldn't contend with someone of his stature for Kelli's affections. He hated to acknowledge that and had mulled over the facts since she returned. He'd always been in love with her.

His expectations were elevated now that she was widowed. Maybe they'd pick up where they left off? He'd never had the same feelings for other women the way he had for Kelli. At one time he was confident she felt the same way, but they were young. Who knew what love really was. But, maybe it could be rekindled?

"Jenn, I'm headed over to the mansion to take another look around. If anyone needs me, you know where I'm at."

"Gotcha," the dispatcher answered.

He strolled to the cruiser like he did at least twenty times a day. Sometimes he wished he'd pursued another occupation, but three generations in his family had been police officers. It was expected.

He couldn't disappoint his paternal grandfather since he raised him from the age of fifteen, after his father went to prison and his mother died a year later of cancer. He swore his mother died of a broken heart after her husband humiliated and disgraced the family. He had taken bribes from local politicians. He abandoned his family, left them in financial and emotional ruin. He'd heard from his father once in a blue moon after he was released from prison. The man had moved away and he had no idea where he was.

Recollections of his estranged father were dreadful. His dad intentionally damaged his self-esteem and teased him at a young age. He was lanky and awkward, physically inept at sports. Since he was the son of the police chief, his father had high expectations for him to follow in his footsteps.

In retaliation, he defied his father and pushed buttons to see how much trouble he could get away with, knowing his father would bail him out only because it affected his reputation. If he couldn't control his son, how could he control a town?

He had been born and raised in Manomet, so it was natural to remain there after graduation, attend junior college, and the police institute. He graduated in the bottom third, but he made it.

As decades passed, he had two failed marriages with no children and dreamt of pursuing a NASCAR career as a pit crew member. He liked grease on his hands and the smell of smoking asphalt. That was one advantage of being a police officer. He could drive faster than the law permitted, no consequences. Plus, people showed him respect, which he never got from his father. He did enjoy meeting people and helping others. It boosted his self-esteem.

His grandfather would have disowned him if he had found out how passionate he was about oil painting and would have viewed his secret hobby as sissified. He'd stare at the ocean for hours, picking unique outdoor scenes to idle away time in the winter and painted them on canvas. His mother framed one of his first paintings which he hid in his closet after she passed. Nobody else cared.

He pulled into the driveway of the mansion. Where did Kelli tell him the key was? Only fifty-three, he sometimes forgot small details. Too much on his mind.

Should be above the double doors on the ledge. He hoped his memory served him well.

Even at six foot he couldn't reach the ledge, so he stood on the wobbly lawn chair long enough to grab the key before it toppled and crushed under his weight.

"Surely, Mr. Rich Man could buy Kelli a new chair," he cursed while he fumbled to unlock the door. The hinges squeaked when it swung open. The house had always made his flesh creep after dark. He only came around because of Kelli since it gave them a place to spend time together.

His investigation yesterday didn't reveal anything. While he strolled up the long staircase, he studied the area for possible clues. He stopped in the doorway to the bedroom where the shot was fired. Kelli's belongings were there, the bed where she slept, her clothes, shoes, and undergarments. He was tempted to sniff. Would that bring back memories from the past? There was a time when he thought they could've had a serious relationship, but one incident on the beach changed everything.

She was the first girl he kissed at the ripe age of fourteen. He remembered the moment like it was yesterday. It was June and a beautiful summer day. After romping on the sandy beach and frolicking in the cold water, he'd spread out a blanket on the sand with another to cover up when the chill set in, which it always did when the sun set behind the bluff.

They plopped on the blanket, fatigued after a full day. He was slightly sunburned on his shoulders. Even though he had a fantastic tan, he was skinny compared to the other boys his age. It'd been a splendid day, no clouds or wind to chop up the clear, nippy water.

Without warning, he scooted closer. She hadn't slipped on her tee shirt to cover her alabaster skin. The purple bikini barely hid her budding breasts. He hardly touched her arm, but it produced goose bumps; his bodily response stunned him.

Warmth stirred from his inner groin, his skin hot and dry. His heartbeat was rapid leaving him unable to catch his breath. He never forgot his first hormonal urge caused by a female presence. What to do, he had wondered, with that strange tangle in his netted trunks?

He startled himself when he leaned in and brushed her salty cheek with his cracked lips. Her reaction indicated surprise. He yearned to touch her bosom, but lack of self-confidence filled both heads, thanks to his dad.

His face was hot, not only from the sunburn, but from physical contact with her delicate lips. No words were exchanged. His second kiss was awkward and overzealous. He braced her back with his sandy hand while he slowly lowered her body on the blanket. Grains of sand embedded in his arm.

Each awkward kiss grew deeper; his tongue twisted, turned, and caught on her metal braces and drew salty blood. He couldn't breathe but was afraid to come up for air and cease the momentum. His lower passion rose.

Was she flustered? She appeared at ease? Maybe she was more experienced than he? He unskillfully slipped his right hand past her belly button. His hand wandered into places he'd never touched on a female. Was she breathing hard too? He slid on top and fumbled to get his other grainy hand up her top in search of a bosom and maybe taut nipples.

Unbeknownst to them, Kelli's father stood at the top of the embankment stairs watching. His manly voice echoed off the bluff and jetties and interrupted what might have been a most eventful day. He didn't mince any bones about his disappointment with the short tryst.

Days afterwards when he came to retrieve Kelli for beach trips, there was awkwardness. He sensed her father didn't trust or like him now, a hard blow given his lack of self-confidence and longing for approval from a father figure. Before he had a chance to mend the relationship, she left to go back to Illinois.

Every summer after that she ignored his calls. Perhaps she was forbidden to be with him by her father.

He was heartbroken, rejected by the first girl he truly cared about. Once he got his driver's license, he dated local gals. Most were easy to satisfy a teenage boy's raging hormones. Plus, he was the son of the police chief, which gave him status which allowed perks.

As they aged and Kelli returned for annual visits, she was polite, but wouldn't give him the time of day. What did he care? His physical needs were being met. His emotional state remained undetermined, unsatisfied. After all these years, was he still crazy about her? Or, was it just unfinished business?

Back to reality, he tucked away memories. His investigation yesterday didn't reveal anything. He sat on

Kelli's bed and imaged her body lying there at night and how marvelous it would be if he were next to her.

He surveyed the hall and room for a bullet casing, but didn't find one. Shattered glass was everywhere. Was this a botched robbery or a failed attempt on Kelli's life? He looked around. What could be worth stealing, anyway?

CHAPTER 30

"Good morning, sunshine," Rod said when Kelli joined him on the stern of his yacht the next morning.

"Sunshine in the morning I'm not, but good try. What time is it?" She squinted from the blinding sun which reflected off the luminous water.

"Quarter after nine. I assume this means you slept well?"

"That's an understatement. You're right about one thing. The gentle rocking of the boat sure helped me sleep. Maybe it was the champagne. Maybe it was you," she joked, obviously uncomfortable about their impromptu love affair last night. "I didn't need my box fan for noise and the waves against the hull were a nice touch."

"Well, so glad I could be of assistance. I think you finally relaxed." He winked, stood up, and placed a kiss on her cheek while he wrapped his arms around her tightly. "Seriously, you can stay as long as you want. It was kinda nice waking up with you next to me."

"I want you to know I don't ever do that. I mean…I don't sleep around with just anyone," she explained. "Thanks for the offer and, not that I don't appreciate your hospitality, but I've got to get down to business on the mansion.

"I need answers. No one's running me off, that's for damn sure. You haven't heard from Gregg Scott, have you?" Her cheek burned from the sensation of his kiss and loved his strong arms. Or was her whole body reliving their sexual escapade? Was she another one night stand for Rod?

"Have a seat, sweetie. Coffee?"

"Yes, cream and sugar."

"Hi-test or decaf?"

"Leaded, please." She wanted to run and hide.

He picked up the phone. "Sy, our guest would like some strong coffee with cream and sugar. Bring the Black Seal too."

She was tense, afraid to gaze into his eyes, even though he had on sunglasses. She wished he'd take them the hell off. She hated sunglasses. No eyes, no soul. Was she so vulnerable she let down her guard and made love with him? She'd never done that, even when she was single. Would she become another trophy girl, another notch on his bed post?

Her heart rate accelerated when she recalled last night. He caressed her back; his sensual touch soothed. He was well endowed, but that wouldn't have mattered. He knew exactly what to do to send her into ecstasy. It'd been a long, long time. She admitted she needed the human connection, more now than ever.

What was there about this man she was drawn to? Her predicament and bad luck? Maybe it was his financial ability to take care of her unlike her husband. Not to mention, he was attractive and had obviously taken good care of himself over the years.

The butler arrived with a carafe of coffee, condiments, pastries, and a bottle. Without glancing at her, Rod filled her cup and then his.

"A splash to ease last evening?" he queried mischievously.

"No way." She giggled nervously.

"I spoke with Officer Scott. We chatted briefly, but they haven't a clue. If they don't come up with something by the end of the week, I'll put my people on it. I have to admit, you're a strong woman with some backbone, Kelli Goddard. Most women would've taken the money and skipped town after what you've been subjected to."

"I'm not most women."

"I know that—now. But speaking of money and running, perhaps you should give my deal more consideration, especially given the incident last night at the mansion."

He took her hand. "Kelli, life's too short. You've already found that out and now to deal with a stressful situation like the mansion. I don't see a realistic chance of you restoring the house on your own. Maybe if you apply for grants, maybe get it on the historical registry, but otherwise, I don't think it can happen.

"It's not realistic for anyone to take on an endeavor of this magnitude. Only a corporation our size or a public agency can afford that place."

She loved the warmth of his hand and how he looked into her eyes when he talked to her. "I understand what you're saying. My financial acumen tells me to run and not look back. My heart insists I stay."

Before he responded, his cell phone rang. He glanced at the screen, swiped it to the left and placed it on the table.

She wondered if he was involved with a woman and wasn't going to answer in front of her.

Why does that bother me? Just because you slept with him doesn't mean you're in love, does it?

"If you need to answer, I can excuse myself," she offered.

"No, it's my father. He can wait." He leaned into her and placed a kiss on her forehead.

He ignited her internal furnace.

Oh my, God. It's way too early for another round. Or is it?

"I hope there are no regrets over last night on your part, but it was marvelous from my point of view," he teased. He placed his hand on her leg.

She fidgeted with the cup, stirred the coffee briskly, swishing coffee onto the saucer. "Rod, last night was a mistake. I was vulnerable. You were available. Don't read anything more into it than what it was. It should have never happened," she lied.

Am I trying to convince myself or give him an out for a fling?

"It wasn't a mistake and you know it. We're two consenting adults, obviously attracted to each other. Making love came natural to both of us. Some things are just meant to be. I don't do one night stands, Kelli, even though you might think so. I've been attracted since I set eyes on you. Granted, we don't come from the same background, but that doesn't make a difference if there's undeniable desire."

"I don't do one-nighters either, but I'm not going to read any more into this than what it was. I needed you last night." She fiddled with the cup. "You didn't have to do what you did to protect me. Thank you for being there. I haven't had someone do that for me in a long time. But, you have no obligation to me."

He reached across the table and melted her lips into his, drawing away her breath.

"Boss, it's your father again. He's insistent you talk to him, like now."

CHAPTER 31

Rod dropped Kelli off at the mansion since he was going to his RV to take care of another business matter.

She rambled around the parlor. Had she complicated her life further and allowed Rod both into her heart and bed last night? Was she ready after five years to start over and give another man a chance?

How could one's life get so screwed up at her age? After they raised their son and worked all those years, it had been time to enjoy life with her husband. Then he died and left his mess for her to clean up.

Can I ever forgive you, Steve?

Sometimes she wanted to punch something, to strike out and make the horrible memories go away. She didn't deserve to have this happen. Their marriage shouldn't have ended this way. She shouldn't have slept with a man she really doesn't know. But she needed it. She'd been deprived enough.

On top of Steve's mess, the burden of the mansion was plopped on her shoulders. Her heart told her to do right by Auntie. Maybe she should take the money and run? Run fast to get away from Rod Kesson.

Millions would make her life stable and secure, something she may never have again if she didn't take his offer. Surely Auntie would understand she had to do this for her son and granddaughters' financial security. And her mental stability.

Now her safety was an issue. That surely should justify her actions.

Her first inclination was Rod might have hired someone to scare her away, but that wasn't possible.

She'd totally misjudged his character, which she normally was pretty good at reading. But, there was the slight chance he might have played on her emotions for the mansion and pretended to be interested in her.

However, she sensed Rod a man of character and integrity. He'd revealed a side she didn't expect when they first met. Not only had he surprised her, but there was an undeniable attraction, similar to how she felt when she met Steve for the first time. Or, was she just lonely, looking for any man who came along?

While sex was incredible with Rod, she was touched by his concern for her well-being and support in time of need, something she desperately craved. She'd never been a needy woman, always independent and able to take care of herself. Her husband encouraged that freedom. But it was different with Steve. They counted on each other. They were partners, for life.

Now, she was alone with no sense of security.

The attraction between her and Rod was undeniable. It was the kind where her insides melted when he looked at her a certain way or touched her at every opportunity, even if a slight rub, a glanced encounter. The playful smile. Staring into each other's eyes for prolonged periods. She couldn't remember the last time someone made her blush like he did.

She craved being with him now, not away. She hadn't experienced that with anyone since her husband. She'd barely dated in the last five years, occasionally going out to appease friends who constantly wanted to fix her up.

Lonely after three years, she tried several on-line dating sites. Every man she dated she compared to her husband and sought out the same physical, emotional, and intellectual attributes.

While she met nice men and one-night losers, it was too time consuming to respond to e-mails and calls. She preferred to devote her time to children who required special attention, the elderly, and her family, especially her granddaughters.

Given the weight of the world on her shoulders, she exhaled and acknowledged the beautiful summer day. It was similar to the carefree, happy summers spent in Manomet with no concerns other than having fun.

Memories were vivid even to this day. Her favorite day of the year was the big celebration held on the third of July. The town and residents labored for weeks and placed small American flags along streets and businesses.

Auntie garnished the mansion with oversized red, white, and blue banners on the wrap-around porch and sewed pads for the weathered white wicker furniture in matching colors.

Almost every home that overlooked the bay had developed a way of getting wood down the bluff to the beach for the bonfire. A tall center pole was buried deep in the rocky sand. Two supporting pieces were nailed to support the wood that was leaned against it. The bonfire was placed strategically so the tide would come in and put out the fire, taking leftover burned wood to sea. Some eventually drifted back in with following tides.

Everyone who had a boat was usually on it. Volleyball and other beach sports were played while boys and men worked hard to build the fire after the permit was up and the fire chief had given the okay.

Families and friends gathered setting up tents, tables, beach chairs, lots of coolers, food, and blankets. Dogs and children romped up and down the beach and occasionally jumped in the clear, cold water or skipped stones. They splashed each other, and their laughter carried up the tall bluff. Finally, the clam bake commenced.

Just before dusk, the huge bonfires were simultaneously lit which set the beach aglow with an orange brightness intense as a sunset. Embers floated effortlessly from the blazes upward and resembled fireflies dancing in the breezes. If they were lucky, embers would drift toward the sea and reflect on the water before drowning.

She'd often climb to the top of the bluff and sit on the slanted built-in seats that had shifted seaward after years of hard weather. An assortment of fireworks illuminated the sky; the scent of smoke lingered. The warmth from the fire reached her, even eighty feet up.

Occasionally a firework display would get out of control, sending screaming and laughing participants in all directions, including into the frigid water. The entire Cape erupted in patriotic celebration; independence prevailed. Every year she was amazed at the beauty of the night, a memory she never wanted to end, an event she never missed. It was like a movie which replayed itself over and over.

Her adult life had now become complicated. She'd never have expected such turmoil at an age when she should be emotionally and financially secure. Her biggest concern should be which warm location to spend winters and what to do in her spare time.

"The golden years," she mused. "Yeah, right."

She moved through the house on auto pilot and wound up in the doorway of her bedroom. A flashback created an explosion that pounded in her ears. Sulfa burned her nose and sinuses, her eyes blinded by the lights when the gun was fired.

Glass was strewn from where the bullet penetrated the window. Still shocked someone tried to shoot her, she wrapped her arms around her shoulders. Chills ran up and down her body. She stroked her arms.

Why me?

"Kelli?" a voice echoed up the stairway.

She listened intently to determine who it was. Her heart pulsated. What if it was the person who tried to shoot her?

"Kelli? You here?"

She moved to the banister and peered over the railing. Gregg Scott stood at the base of the stairs.

"Gregg, come on in. You scared me to death." She clutched her chest while descending the stairs.

"Sorry. Hope I'm not interrupting."

"No, not at all. Just surveyed the damage upstairs. Did you guys find out anything?"

"Unfortunately, no. The only evidence was the shattered glass. We'll never find the bullet, probably outside somewhere in the overgrown brush. No casing was found inside."

She plopped down on the long lounger in the parlor. Her finger traced the raised gold velvet. "What's your gut feeling? Is someone trying to scare the shit out of me? I'll admit, it's made a dent in my decision to stay. I'm a determined woman, but I've just about had enough. How much can one person take?"

Gregg pulled up a tall wooden chair next to her. He stroked her arm. His intimacy surprised her. She recoiled, ever so slightly. He appeared not to notice.

"I wouldn't try to influence your decision one way or the other, but with everything you've gone through, I'd take a suggestion from a long-time friend and get out of Manomet."

"I've got to admit I'm surprised to hear you say that. I thought you'd be the one person to encourage me to stay." Gregg, of all people, should understand how she cherished this home and memories.

"Normally I would. But sometimes we reach a point of no return. Where are you going to come up with the money to restore much less keep up on long-term maintenance costs, taxes, and all the rest of the expenses?

"It's going to cost millions to do that, Kelli. You might be able to get grants or historical preservation funding to help, but that's a shit load of work. Sure, Hattie wanted to keep it in the family, but even Hattie couldn't maintain it. Don't let the past keep you from embracing the future."

"Hattie did fine until she got sick. She would've never allowed it to get in this condition. I'm confused and overwhelmed right now." A tear dripped off her jowl.

"No one can make this decision for you, but there's no way you can do this alone." He moved closer and wrapped his arm around her shaking shoulder. "If you want, I could—"

"She's not alone," a voice carried from the hall. Rod stepped into the parlor.

"What?" Gregg asked.

"I said she's not alone. With my resources, we can restore this house."

Gregg rose and stepped to within inches of Rod's face. "No one invited you in this conversation, or actually, even into this house. This conversation is between me and Kelli, so I suggest you turn around and leave before I have to throw you out."

"Nope, not leaving unless Kelli wants me to. Kelli?"

"Oh, come on. Guys, I can't handle all this testosterone right now. Why don't you both give me some space? I just need time to think this through by myself. Can you understand that? I'm not trying to be rude or anything, but I just need to have some time to myself."

"You sure you want to be alone?" Rod inquired.

"Yes, please. I need to sort all this out. Thanks to both of you, but we'll chat later." She showed the men to the door.

Words were exchanged which she couldn't hear while they got into their respective vehicles. She guessed they weren't headed to the Moose for a beer together.

All she wanted was two aspirins to stop the approaching migraine—and peace. She laid on the long chaise and closed her eyes and took deep breaths.

A small hand caressed her hair. A lock was being twirled in someone's fingers. She opened her eyes. A young woman was close; her features were more distinct than before. Her face was pasty pale and eyes without shine. The blonde hair's sheen was so slick it appeared she'd overused Mongolian oil. It draped over one shoulder and breast.

She pulled off a white glove which disclosed long but dainty fingers. The pink satin dress had a wide white ribbon at the waist. A delicate gold locket hung from her elongated neck.

Next to her on the floor was a rare antique baby doll. Her hair had been pulled away which exposed a beige band. Its face was still perfect, eyebrows lined in brown, painted black eyelashes, and red perfect cherub lips. The long-sleeved rust dress covered most of the off-white socks and black patent shoes. An orange bow was tacked in the middle.

"You have to help Joshua find his way to me," the spirit whispered. "He can't get out. He has to be released. Please help my love. You are in grave danger, but I will protect you. Our spirits are kindred through the loss of our loved ones. Your husband passed over, but asked me to keep you safe. He said he was sorry. He never meant for you to be hurt. He loved you."

The apparition picked up the doll and toyed with its matted hair. "My father was a mean man. He lied to me. Joshua didn't die at sea. He needs to come home to me. Help him. Please help us. I will help you."

CHAPTER 32

Drained from the morning's events, Kelli woke from a brief nap still lying on the antique divan. Had she dreamed the ghost talked to her?

Unsettled, it was too radiant outside to not stroll parts of the property she hadn't seen since her return. Unfortunately, most of the acreage had become overgrown by suckers of Norway maples, cedars, oaks, and thickets of wild honeysuckle.

She sauntered in the opposite direction of the bluff into the thickset forest. Overhanging branches formed a solid canopy and only allowed beams of sun through which created a green haze. Bittersweet vines made it difficult to maneuver through the debris. Sizable limbs caused her to stumble.

Rampant thoughts from the last few days raced through her mind. She hadn't noticed how far away she was from the mansion until a rabbit jumped from its hiding place, scurried into the distance, and jumped across a mossy knoll.

Auntie occasionally brought her on this side of the estate when she searched for wild ferns to repot for the porch in the summer. Auntie had told her the Eldridge family cemetery plot was over here, but she couldn't remember where.

The unnatural hump was probably dirt from an old well that had been filled in over the years. Located far from the house, hopefully, it wouldn't require removal which would be costly. She hadn't given consideration to the acreage and its needs, totally focused on the mansion's problems.

A shiny gold object on top of the knoll flickered from the sunlight. Only half exposed, she dug it out of the dirt. It was a gold band, a wedding ring. Without warning, loose ground under her feet gave way. Her body tossed sideways and downward into a deep hole. Rough damp stones caught her clothes and tore exposed skin while she made the descent.

When she hit bottom, pressure pushed on her lungs. She couldn't breathe and was blinded temporarily. Blood dripped from a head wound and streamed into her eyes and mouth, gagging her with bitterness.

She searched with her right hand. The space wasn't big but filled with debris. Had she fallen into a well? She struggled to move in the tight catacomb. Her claustrophobia caused her chest to tighten.

"Help. Can anyone hear me?" she yelled.

Her voice reverberated off the mossy walls. Her eyes adjusted to darkness. Verdant trees, shadows swayed over her eyes to the sky.

"Can anyone hear me? Help," she cried louder.

No one was on the property. The probability of someone finding her was next to nil. She cried in frustration, not believing another catastrophic event had befallen her.

She shut her eyes to regroup her mental composure. When she shuffled, her palm was poked by a pointed object which was sleek and smooth, partially covered in dirt. She cringed when she thought what might be in the hole. Was it the carcass of an animal? What if snakes or spiders were there? She shook her shoulders.

Hours seemed like days. She cried and yelled while she attempted to shimmy up the shaft, but couldn't get a grip on the wet stones which tore her fingertips.

I can't believe this is happening, damn it. It's like I was destined to fail the minute I walked back on this property. Is this how my life is going to end, in a deep hole where no one will ever find me?

God, I need you now more than ever. Not for me, but for my family. I want to see my granddaughters grow up and be part of their lives.

Have I asked too much of you in the last five years? If so, I'm sorry. You are my guidance. You're the one who helped me through Steve's death. I figured it was your higher powers that made these decisions. He didn't deserve to die. I was mad at you for a long time, but I thought we had that resolved.

She laughed through streaming droplets and sat there quietly for a few moments until the finality of her situation set in.

I pray you'll spare my life. But if you don't, I am prepared to go with you when you're ready. Knowing this is your calling, I accept whatever my fate is.

At her lowest emotionally and considering the consequences and impact of her demise on her family and friends, she quietly sobbed. Suddenly, an illuminated ultramarine haze congealed in the cavity.

"You found the wedding ring I was going to give Belinda on the night they killed me. It led you to me. Now that you have found and released me from my grave, I will release you. Know Sam Eldridge killed me," the man's voice said softly, without anger.

Had she suffered a concussion? Was she delirious? Had a ball of light spoke to her?

"Captain Eldridge could not bear the thought of the two of us together. He tricked me into coming to the woods to reason with me, or so he said. He'd been drinking and was on a rampage. He offered me money to leave town and never come back. I would never leave my Belinda. When I walked away, he shot me in the back. Kent witnessed it.

"Eldridge forced Kent to throw me in the well and cover the hole with limbs and debris. I was mortally wounded. He buried me alive because of the love I shared with his daughter. Now we can both be released."

She was not given time to decipher the intellectual message. Her body was hoisted by an unknown force up through the walls and onto the ground above. Her head reeled. She fainted.

When she woke next to the deep hole, her body was covered in dirt and stained with blood. A gold band was in her palm.

CHAPTER 33

"You dumb shit," Bubba Smithe announced from his barstool. "I give you one fuckin' job to do and you can't even get that done right. What in the hell were ya thinking?"

"Hey, asshole. You're the one that fucked up. If you'd scared Kelli away the first time, I wouldn't have had to fire a bullet to freak her out," Johnny protested. "Or go out on that skiff and almost get run over by a damn yacht in the middle of the night. We were no match for that size yacht, even with the shotguns and flares. Your plans suck."

"Well, you know what this means, don't ya?" Bubba asked.

"What the hell, now?" Johnny answered.

"We're going with Plan B which we sure as hell didn't want to do."

"Shit, Bubba. I'm not doing it. Ya're on your own. It's a wonder we haven't been caught so far. No way in hell am I doing it. We're both on probation and if we get caught screwing up again, we're in the slammer for a long time."

"No way, dude, you're backing out now. Ya ain't got no choice. Either we get this lady out of that mansion or it won't matter anyway. We'll be dead meat. We're faced with the worst of two evils, and I'd deal with her over the other any day. He said he'd kill us and I have no doubt he will. Okay, shithead, listen up for a change. Pick me up at nine tonight."

"Man, I don't think I can go through with this."

"We're not going to hurt her, we're gonna scare her shitless this time. She'll definitely leave town. Then we can get into the house, find the coins, and we're outta here. I've got my wish list, baby."

They clinked Sam Adams beer bottles in celebration of the upcoming windfall.

They went to their respective run-down shacks. Most residents in this small community would never have entered their homes, not up to their higher standards. His was probably the worst of the two since he never threw out anything. His lawn looked like a salvage yard. Old trucks, boats, and motorcycles lined the driveway and were stacked against the side of the peeling house.

Johnny pulled up a few minutes before nine in the alley with everything in the trunk he'd been instructed to bring: black ski mask, hoody, duct tape, rope, bandana, flashlight, chloroform, rag, and knife. In the duffel bag he had prepared the handwritten note they'd leave at the scene which would indicate Kelli had enough and left town. The thirty-seven revolver weighed down the tote.

"Don't fuckin' believe it. You're on time for once in your life, dude," Bubba joked while he threw his bag in the back seat.

"I'm serious, man. I can't do this," Johnny whined.

"Well guess what? We're on our way to being so stinkin' rich we won't know what to do with all the money. Our toys will put Kesson's to shame. We'll see how the ladies like us then."

As planned, they parked the corroded eighty-four Chevy a block from the mansion. The muffler had rusted apart years ago and made it noisy. They were concerned it might attract attention. By doing their heist at that time of evening, there was plenty of traffic to distract local residents who were used to kids hot rodding.

To their advantage, they knew the neighborhood like the back of their hand. They'd lived in Manomet all their lives, riding bikes and scooters in the cart path behind the mansion. Hattie had sold off five acres behind the house so it could be developed into housing for the elderly. The aged residents couldn't hear well or didn't worry about crime or loud noises since they were usually in bed by eight-thirty.

"Right over there. Park in the path under that large oak," he instructed.

Johnny shut off the lights and engine and cruised into the overgrown way. Gravel crunched under the tires. They jumped out simultaneously. Johnny unlocked the trunk, slipped on his hoody, and left the ski mask and other items in the small duffle.

Bubba stuck his hand in his bag and grabbed his jacket. "Okay, ready? You follow my lead and do exactly what I tell you. Just like we planned."

"I'm tellin' ya, dude, I got a bad feelin' 'bout this."

"Fuckin' get over it."

They slowly made their way down the path and crept along the backyards of the houses. The uncontrolled foliage was their friend tonight along with the clouded sky, which made it darker than normal.

When they reached the rear of the house, they surveyed the driveway to make sure only Kelli's Jeep was there. A light glow came from the upstairs bedroom, the one he'd fired the shot into. He had no intent on killing, only to scare her away. That didn't work. Hopefully, this plan would.

Everything was going like clockwork. They carefully removed the piece of plywood dislodged the other night before setting the fire. They propped it against the foundation of boulders where it could be replaced in a hurry. They now had easy access to the entrance through the basement.

A dog barked which caused Bubba to spot his jeans. They turned off the flashlight in case someone happened by. He'd always been the ring leader. Johnny was the tail man doing mostly dirty work and when he banged his foot into a stray piece of wood, it gave away his buddy had downed a few more beers than usual.

"Dammit, be quiet, you clumsy ox," he scolded.

Bent at the waist since that part of the basement was only four foot, they made their way through the north passage. Once in the main basement, they stood and turned on the flashlights. He was familiar with the layout of the house.

With three-foot wide slabs of granite, no wonder the house had remained stable and structurally sound all these years. A lot of houses on the bluff had been mangled beyond repair over time by nasty winters and high winds during hurricanes and nor'easters, but not this one.

Old coal crunched under their boots. The beam flashed into the coal chute and bin.

"Did ya see that," Johnny whispered as he backed into an old door against a brick wall.

"Be quiet. What?"

"That blue light over there in the corner. It moved." Johnny's voice quivered.

"There's no blue light and shut the hell up. She's gonna hear us."

The basement had many compartments, a main room and side sections. An alcove housed an old toilet with the water tank above, both disgustingly rusted and nasty. Exposed light bulbs dangled from wires on the ceiling. They slowly advanced up the narrow steps and attempted to avoid spider webs that'd made a home since their last visit.

Johnny tripped on a step. "Sorry."

"Sorry, my ass. Keep it up and you'll blow this," he chastised.

When they reached the top step into the kitchen, he stopped and stuck his head out to make sure Kelli wasn't downstairs. He assumed she was in her bedroom since that was the only room which reflected light from the outside.

They tiptoed quietly through the kitchen to the servant stairs at the back of the house which led to the second floor. He climbed the stairs while Johnny slipped down the main corridor next to the grand staircase. The back stairs were by far narrower but certainly came in handy for their attack and escape tonight.

He held his breath with each step. When he reached the landing, he stopped and listened. Soft music of chirping birds floated throughout the house.

A door separated the back of the house from the front. He opened it slowly and grimaced, afraid it'd creak. He peeked down the long hallway. A flash of blue light caught his attention in the wrought iron grate between the floors. A faint glow illuminated the wood floor outside her bedroom. He slipped on his ski mask.

As planned, Johnny slinked his way down the main hall and rapped his knuckles on the heavy front door to gain Kelli's attention, then stepped behind the vestibule door.

Kelli rustled in the room. Barefoot, she emerged and strolled to the top of the staircase and stopped.

Bubba drew in a deep breath and pounced with the soaked rag of chloroform in his glove. Because of the darkness and speed, he caught Kelli off-guard. He grabbed her from behind and placed the rag over her nose and mouth.

She struggled and screamed; her fingernails dug into his arms. Thirty seconds later the chemical rendered her unconscious. Once she was limp in his arms, he lowered her to the floor.

"Johnny, she's out. Get up here," he yelled down the stairs.

Johnny bounded up the risers two at a time guided by his flashlight.

"Quick. Grab her feet. I'll get her hands," he instructed.

"Damn man, I don't believe we're doing this."

"Shut the hell up and do what you're told."

Together they moved her limp body to the back of the house and up an even smaller set of stairs to the third floor where short ceilings were accented by angled walls. The rooms appeared to close in on him, which made it hard to breathe.

Winded and fatigued from her dead weight, they arrived at the short third staircase. They placed her flimsy body on the landing while he opened the bulky hatch and used his damaged shoulder for leverage. A full moon illuminated the staircase and Mansard roof.

"Grab her feet, asshole. Let's get her up here and get this done," he instructed.

They maneuvered the body up the staircase, huffing and puffing to get her petite frame through the small hatch and onto the badly damaged roof. Bubba was the first to step out. The fresh air aided his breathing. Three stories high made him dizzy and unsteady.

"Keep pulling. She's almost up," Johnny said.

With one final push, Kelli's unconscious body laid on top of the severely damaged widow's walk. They tore off ski masks and wiped sweat created from their toil. Bubba leaned against the badly decomposed wrought iron railing. It rattled and shifted.

"Man, I don't dig it up here," Johnny remarked.

"You don't have to dig anything. Let's get this over with and get the hell out of town."

"Get what over with?"

"Let's dump her over the railing. It'll look like a suicide."

"What the fuck? That wasn't the plan?"

"Well, guess what, you stupid shit? The plan just changed. We can't take a chance this will scare the shit out of her and she'll leave town. We both know that. Look at all the other things we've done and it hasn't scared her off."

"But—"

"But nothing. Shut the fuck up and help me lift her."

"Won't do it. I'm no murderer." Johnny backed down the stairs.

"Yes, you will and you better get your ass back up here, or you'll be going over the side with her."

Before Johnny responded, a phosphorescent circular blue glow appeared. It sliced through his body which caused him to fall backwards, down the stairs.

Bubba's chest squeezed; he couldn't catch his breath again. The blue mist cast a form of a man who stood at the end of the widow's walk.

"What the hell?"

The vapor floated towards him, causing him to trip over Kelli's body. He backed away and into the rusty railing. It groaned and buckled under the weight of his body.

Fear encapsulated him. He had no control. His body slid down the roof. His hands grasped at anything to break his fall. Broken sharp slate shingles ripped through his palms which skinned his fingers and fingernails. When he was about to plunge over the side, his right hand grabbed a finial which slowed his descent.

While the full moon illuminated the roof and tops of the trees, the misty outline hovered above the widow's walk. The iridescent form glided towards him. His fingers slipped one at a time. Terror enveloped him. The mist hovered directly over his body, close enough cold eyes pierced into his.

Without warning, it peeled one finger at a time from his only lifeline. He fought with all his strength. The descent from three stories appeared to take hours before his body hit the hard ground.

CHAPTER 34

Rod called Kelli several times. When she didn't answer, he sensed something was amiss. At nine-thirty on Thursday night, he couldn't imagine where she might be unless Officer Scott had shown up. She still would have answered her phone.

Rampant thoughts overwhelmed him. He was concerned for her safety and realized how much he cared about this woman. Was she the real deal? Could he be in love with someone he'd known so briefly? He'd never felt so emotionally attached to anyone in his life, except his mother.

He jumped into his truck and drove to the mansion. When he pulled up, the only light on was in her bedroom. When he made his way to the front door, he immediately noticed something lying in the tall grass. When he got closer, he discovered a man face down in the undergrowth. He placed two fingers on his neck, which was still warm, and checked for a pulse. Dead. Not anyone he recognized.

"Kelli, what's going on?" he yelled panic stricken. He pulled his cell phone from his pocket and dialed nine-one-one.

"What's your emergency?"

"I'm at the Manomet Mansion. There's a body in the front yard. This is Rod Kesson. I'm going into the house to see if Kelli Goddard is all right. Please send an ambulance and police." He stuck the phone in his pant pocket while he ran up the wobbly steps to the open front door.

"Kelli, are you okay?" he shouted. His voice echoed throughout the house.

No answer. Even though dark inside, the full moon's radiance shone through the smudged windows. He bolted up the staircase to her bedroom. She wasn't there.

"Kelli, where are you?"

A thump echoed from the third floor. He probed his way to the back of the house to find a staircase and quickly climbed, missing a step and banging his knee.

"Kelli? Are you here?" he clamored louder.

Another thud reverberated through the empty house. He followed the noise down a long hallway to another set of stairs. A bright light illuminated the staircase, so he quickly climbed the short boards to the roof.

Kelli was on her side and stirred slightly.

"Kelli, you all right? What happened?" He picked her up, her torso flimsy like a rag doll. She groaned, but didn't open her eyes.

He stuck his hand in his pants to retrieve his phone, but it was gone. Shit. He must have missed his pocket in his haste to get into the house, probably in the front yard by the body. He knelt down and positioned his arms under her shoulders and knees to lift her.

"No need to do that, Mr. Kesson," a voice called from the top of the stairs.

"Help. She needs help, she's hurt."

"Yes, I think she needs help, but I don't think you're going to be the one to do it. Actually, I think you're a bad boy and you're going to hurt her," the voice explained from the dark.

"Who are you?" he demanded.

The man emerged from the shadow and moved to the top step where the full moon cast shadows on his face, its brilliance reflected off his shiny badge.

"Officer Scott?" he asked in disbelief.

"No, but I know Gregg well. He's my son."

"Don't stand there. Give me a hand. Kelli's hurt and someone's dead on the lawn."

"You know, if you hadn't of fucked up our plan, no one would've gotten hurt."

"What are you talking about? Are you out of your mind?"

"Oh, no. Quite the contrary. You see, I always liked Kelli. Actually had hoped someday she might marry my son and inherit the house from Hattie. Maybe then none of this would have happened.

"Since I got kicked off the force and banned from town, my life's been a living hell. I became the laughingstock. Sometimes desperate times create desperate measures. Time to call in all the favors I did for everyone over the years.

"Bubba and Johnny were indebted to me. I kept those boys from going to jail more times than even I want to keep track of. Neither one had a lick of sense. They did all my dirty work trying to scare away Kelli."

"You're insane. I'll give you whatever you want, but we have to help Kelli," he pleaded.

"Aren't you the knight in shining armor? When I heard your company was planning to tear down the mansion, I had to take action. It wasn't fair you'd come in and take millions in silver and coins ole' Captain Eldridge stashed.

"You weren't interested in developing condominiums, were you? You knew about the treasure. That's what your company was after from the get go, wasn't it? Thought you'd get the girl in the process too, I bet."

"You son of a bitch, you've lost it. The most important thing right now is for us to get Kelli help. If it's money you want, you've got it."

"She won't feel a thing. Chloroform's going to wear off, but the bullet will kill her. Just like poor Bubba down there. Afraid I'll have to drag Johnny's ass up here and dump him too. Or maybe I'll make you do it before I kill you."

"So, you're the one behind what's been happening to Kelli all along? You'd kill for a little money?"

"Little?" Adam Scott laughed. "You have no idea. Yes, I'm entitled. Hoped she'd reconnect with Gregg and lead him to the coins. Got nothing to lose anymore. Spent time in prison, lost my family, respect, job. I deserve to be compensated for all my years of service. They kicked me out with no severance, nothing in return for me risking my life day after day for over thirty years. Took away my pension. Basically left me destitute.

"If I've got to be miserable, might as well be wealthy and spend my life in some tropical countryside. Someone had to find the coins. And that someone is gonna be me."

"Okay, that's enough." He stood up quickly which caused him to wobble. He stepped towards the man he'd never met before now.

"Whoa, buddy. Not a step further. See, here's how it's gonna play out for the police. They find Bubba and you dead on the lawn from an apparent fall from the widow's walk after a struggle. The gun has your fingerprints. Kelli and Johnny are on the third floor landing, dead from gunshot wounds.

"The investigators think you whacked everyone because Kelli wouldn't give in to your threats and sell the house to you. They won't give much consideration to Bubba and Johnny since they've always been in trouble and have a police record a mile long. It'd sure been one hell of a lot longer if I hadn't taken care of those boys.

"They'll probably figure you paid them to scare Kelli off. When it was time to pay up, you killed them instead. You greedy bastard. Like you and your family don't already have enough wealth and prestige."

"You son of a bitch." Rod wanted to push the crazy old man over the edge, but had a gun pointed at him.

"Quite the tragedy and uproar for such a small village. Of course, no one will ever know I was the mastermind behind the plan since my accomplices, you, and Kelli will be dead. They never gave me enough credit when I was the chief. Never got the respect I deserved. They quickly forgot how much I'd sacrificed to take care of this town and village."

"You'll never get away with this."

A crimson mist appeared quickly turning solid. A young woman with blonde hair was dressed in a long red satin gown, her slender hands adorned with white gloves.

Adam Scott's eyes bulged. The female remained directly in front of him, so close he had no place to go other than back down the stairs.

"You...you knew," the ghostly figured wailed. "You knew all along my father killed Joshua. He made my brother throw Joshua down the old well leaving his body never to be discovered. Then my brother committed suicide, unable to live with what he did, unable to reveal the truth against my father. You found my father's journal in the attic when you searched for the coins. You could've revealed the truth and set Joshua free," she cried.

"What the hell?" Adam Scott blurted out. He gradually backed up and tripped down the stairs and stumbled over Johnny's body on the landing, righting himself. He bolted down the hall. The spirit glided effortlessly down the stairs, over Johnny's body and followed him.

Kelli's hand moved. She came to. Rod slid his arms under her and carried her down the stairs. He stepped over Johnny.

Footsteps and eerie screams echoed throughout the house while he laid her on the floor. Approaching sirens reverberated in the far distance.

He followed the sounds down the back stairs to the resplendent red light on the second floor. An ear-piercing scream was followed by splintering of wood.

CHAPTER 35

Gregg arrived at the mansion in seven minutes after getting the dispatch. The New England Clam Bake was in full swing. Given past celebrations, every police officer had been assigned since they'd had their share of over served patrons to deal with in the past.

Police lights strobed the area. He jumped out of the cruiser before it had barely come to a halt. Was someone trying to harm Kelli again? He darted into the house and almost stumbled over a body on the lawn. Bubba was dead.

His throat caught. Where was Kelli? Gun drawn and flashlight propped in his left hand, he flashed the beam back and forth. "Kelli, are you here?"

Commotion echoed above. Someone was fleeing down the back stairs. He slinked against the entry wall, his weapon steady in his hand. He had the advantage since he knew the layout of the house, and he carried the blinding light.

Perfectly still, he tried not to breathe loudly. Whoever was coming towards him wouldn't have a chance since he was an acclaimed marksman. He tried to suppress the cough that welled in his chest.

A dark figure came around the corner and approached quickly. With his finger on the trigger, he was ready to pull.

"Police. Stop or I'll shoot," he yelled.

The target continued to move in his direction. The trigger released. The bullet sped toward the shape. Instantaneously, a red mist moved the dark figure out of the path of the oncoming bullet. Time warped. The

235

person fell to the floor. The bullet lodged into old wood and thudded at its resting place.

"It's me, Rod Kesson. Don't shoot," the voice bellowed. Rod was on the floor shielding his eyes from the flashlight.

"Kesson, turn over and put your hands behind your head," he yelled.

"What the hell? Hey, I'm not your guy. Kelli's hurt upstairs."

He inched closer, his eyes had adjusted to the darkness, even though the flash from the firing of the gun lingered.

"Stay down and I mean now." From years of training, he knelt down and forced his weight onto Rod's middle back. He unhitched the handcuffs and snapped them tightly around the man's wrists, pulling him to a standing position.

"The guy you're looking for ran this way. He might have fallen. Let go of me and get him. Kelli's unconscious upstairs."

None of it made sense. He wanted to check on Kelli but had to check out Kesson's story in case the perp was hiding. Or was it a ploy to buy Rod time?

"Stay right here and don't move." He inched his way into the large dark parlor. Only his flashlight gave assistance. The beam spotted broken wood and plaster dangled from the ceiling. When he inched closer, he spotted a motionless body under the debris. His arm ached from holding the gun and arm in firing position, but he didn't let down his guard.

He kicked pieces of wood off the body to see if it moved. It didn't. A boot was exposed, so he touched it. Nothing.

Staying away from striking distance, he lowered himself on one knee and shined the light on the bloody distorted face. Afraid the person was playing possum, he waited for him to strike.

"Oh my, God," he bellowed.

It was his father.

CHAPTER 36

Kelli woke in a daze, confused by her surroundings. It didn't take long to realize she was on the yacht, Rod curled up next to her.

Was that a nightmare last night? Scott's dad died. He was the one who tried to harm me?

A teardrop slid down her face; her soul ached. How could she be wrong about so many people in her life? Her husband and now an old friend's father had tried to hurt her, all over money. What a shame he'd betrayed his son.

She studied Rod's smooth, muscled body while he snuggled closer, wrapping his arm around her waist. She never thought she could believe in another man again. Her heart declared she could trust Rod. She stared at his face, blessed and grateful for a man whose actions proved he truly cared. Had she fallen in love again?

Her heart had been broken into so many pieces when Steve died. But the tragedy became worse when she found out he hadn't loved her enough to trust her with the truth. Or, was it the opposite?

During their heart-wrenching discussions until the wee hours, Rod pointed out that perhaps Steve had loved her so much that he tried to fix the problem before she found out. Now that Rod was in her life, her grief and anger had lifted. She perceived life from a different, more rational, and positive perspective. They were able to talk about everything, her problems as well as his with his father.

They were a match made in heaven. When they'd chat for hours, they stared into each other's eyes while talking about intimate details she hadn't been able to discuss since Steve's death.

Her cell phone rang. It startled her and woke Rod.

"Hello," she whispered.

"Kelli Goddard?"

"Yes. Who's calling?"

"It's Linda McLean. I'm an ICU nurse at Jordan Hospital in Plymouth. Captain Mazalewski has been admitted. He's had a heart attack and gave us your name to contact."

"Sam had another heart attack? When? Is he going to be okay?"

"About an hour ago. They've been working on him. He's stable and alert, but asked we call you."

"I'll be right there," she responded. She couldn't catch her breath.

Rod sat up in bed and ran his fingers through his rumpled hair. "What's wrong?"

"Sam's had a heart attack. I've got to get to the hospital. Can you get me there? I can't believe this. When will all this madness stop?"

He leaped out of bed and grabbed his phone. "Get my car ready. We need to get to the hospital ASAP, like pronto." They scurried down the boardwalk to the car that had pulled up to the gated area of the marina.

On arrival they were led into the intensive care unit where only Kelli was allowed, against Rod's protest. Her stomach roiled by the sight of Sam with hoses and tubes running from his nose and arms.

She placed a kiss on his aged sweaty forehead. "Captain Maz, what happened?"

"Reckon this ole' codger's lifestyle finally caught up with me again. Guess ya can't eat butter and lobsta all yar life without cloggin' up yar arteries." He attempted a joke and coughed. "Think they're going to have to put in some of those stents to open up these old veins. Thought after the open heart surgery I'd be good to go for at least fifty years."

"I'm sorry you have to go through this. Is there anything I can do to help?"

"No, sweet pea. But grab a seat. I want to talk to ya seriously about something before surgery, in case I don't make it out."

"Don't you dare talk like that." She grabbed the heavy leather chair and pulled it close to the hospital bed.

She clutched his cold hand and patted it. "What? What can I do for you? I'd do anything in the world. I hope you know that." Overwhelmed with emotion, she swallowed against her tightened throat.

"I should've told ya when ya were over at the house. I want ya to know my first priority was to keep ya safe. Always know that."

"Okay, but what are you talking about? You're confusing me."

"Hattie made me swear I wouldn't tell ya until I thought it was the right time. I've tried several times, but we kept getting interrupted. I'd made up my mind and then this damn ole' heart acted up again. You've been through so much, Kelli." He weakly squeezed her hand. "Imagine this will come as a great shock. Hattie wanted to tell you before she got sick, but ya lost your husband and had enough stress on your plate."

"Yeah?"

"Remember yar mother and Hattie had issues all of a sudden?"

"I always wondered why and no one would ever tell me. Mom and Dad refused to discuss it."

"There's a good reason. We can talk in more detail when I get out of this place, but, Kelli…." His hand shook while he held hers tightly. "Hattie was yar biological mother."

Her purse dropped off her lap, its contents spilling out. She stopped breathing.

"Kelli, ya okay?" He tightened his grip.

"What? That can't be? How can that be possible?"

"It's a pretty long and complicated story, but Hattie was with child out of wedlock. Yar parents tried to have children for years. Yar mother couldn't conceive.

"Seemed like a perfect solution for the two sisters. Hattie was too young to raise a child alone. Yar mother was devastated she couldn't bear children. Hattie loved ya enough she wanted ya to have a life she couldn't give ya. Her father would have disowned her if she'd kept ya. So…yar mother and father legally adopted ya."

"I don't believe it. Can't be?" She wailed.

"Why do ya think ya got to come every summer? Hattie insisted. When ya got older, Hattie wanted to tell ya the truth and raise ya, but yar parents wouldn't have anything to do with it, especially after they lost your brother in the car accident. He was adopted too."

She was confused and dumbfounded.

"I can't believe this. Why wouldn't they have told us? So, Blake wasn't my biological brother?"

"No, honey, he wasn't. Hidden in a big trunk on the third floor is yar birth certificate along with precious memories Hattie saved for ya in case something happened to her. She taped the key to a shelf in the china cabinet."

"I found that key by accident. I can't believe this."

"Know this is a lot to digest. She'd planned to tell ya herself, but she got sick and didn't want ya to be obligated to take care of her. She knew ya struggled with yar own demons with yar husband's death and affairs. She was fearful ya'd hate her for not being truthful with ya."

"Hate her? Hattie my mother? I always loved her."

"And I might as well get it all out jus' in case I don't make it through this damn surgery. There's one more thing."

She wrung her hands. Tears trickled down her cheeks.

"Yar father. I'm sure that's yar next question. Well, I can't prove one hundred percent, but I think I'm your father, Kelli. Hattie and I had been free spirits for quite a while before ya were born. She kept her pregnancy a secret from everyone.

"She went to Illinois for a while to go to college and lived with her sister. She didn't admit all this until she got sick with Alzheimer's. Kept it bottled up all those years. Thought she was protecting both of us. I never had a chance to find out for sure and that's how Hattie wanted it."

"You, my father?" Tears cascaded down her face and nose.

"If you want, after I get done with this operation, we can have a blood test done. Then we'll both know for sure. I think it's time to get all these secrets out in the open. It's a long time overdue. Sure wish it could've happened when Hattie was alive and the two of you enjoy the time left."

"I can't believe this. It's surreal." She pushed her undone hair out of her eyes.

"And one more."

She stood up. "I can't take one more."

"You need to sit and listen, Kelli. This is very important. The rumors about Captain Eldridge hiding silver and coins in the mansion are true. Also, in the old locked trunk ya'll find a wrinkled old paper in a book that had interior pages cut out. It holds a map.

"It'll show ya the locations in the Mansard where the coins are hidden. When ya go up the stairs to the widow's walk, there's a small door next to the landing. That's how ya get into the Mansard attic. There are hidden, shallow halls.

"Don't ya do it, but Rod or one of his workers can check it out. Stay on the boards, but on the back side of each fireplace are loose bricks. That's where the coins are hidden. Should be three spots.

"Now mind ya, and don't think I've gone loony, but Hattie said Belinda gave her the map drawn by Captain Eldridge. Hattie never had to look for coins. Belinda knew where they were and gave to Hattie every time she ran out of money. Yes, it's unequivocally true. Belinda exists."

Dumbfounded and shocked, she had trouble comprehending these secrets—and lies. A ghost gave a treasure map to Auntie—her mother—supposedly hidden by Captain Eldridge in the late 1800's?

Hattie's my mother and Captain Maz my father?

She fainted.

CHAPTER 37

The morning had been stressful. First, Kelli visited Captain Maz at the hospital and anxiously waited while he had surgery. And then the earth-shattering revelations. She couldn't grasp the fact Hattie was her biological mother and Captain Maz possibly her father? It all made sense now. Growing up, there were several times she needed a birth certificate. When she asked her mother for it, she hesitated and appeared rattled.

And to boot, she might have inherited millions in coins? Was that why Auntie had been adamant to keep the property for generations? The more she thought about all that had happened in the past, the puzzle made sense now.

Hattie wanted the mansion to stay intact for her—her daughter. Which meant, Hattie had a grandson and great granddaughters. She wanted the house handed down to them too.

Captain Maz's stent operation was successful. They put in two on the right and one on the left. He was ordered to be on a restricted diet for the rest of life, but she doubted he'd adhere to anything doctors instructed. He was stubborn. If he hadn't done it before, he wasn't going to start now. She could see Hattie's traits in herself and prayed Captain Maz was her father.

As for finding the treasure, even though a map supposedly existed, she wasn't going to count her chickens before they hatched. It'd be awesome if collectible coins were found and appraised, giving her funds to restore the mansion. But according to Rod, her funds were immaterial. He was sticking around because of her and going to pay for the restoration of the mansion.

Auntie would be smiling down for sure. Maybe her luck had finally taken a turn.

She spent most of the morning with Rod at the police station being interviewed about last night. Details were difficult to remember due to her unconsciousness from the chloroform.

They were informed during the interrogation Officer Gregg Scott had been put on a paid leave of absence for multiple reasons, but the chief didn't go into detail. Gregg had passed the polygraph and been cleared of any involvement in his father's scheme. Since his father was killed and involved in the attempted murder of Kelli, they didn't want Gregg in the department until Internal Affairs had done a thorough investigation.

Her heart weighed heavily for her old friend, Gregg. He'd had a hard life. His father destroyed the family because of his greed. Now, not only was his mother gone, so was his father.

Exhausted by the strain from the long multiple interviews and happenings the night before, they left the station. Rod opened the truck's door, and she slid in.

"Well, after last night and this morning, what do you think we should do for adventure? It's going to be hard to top all of this?" he asked.

She wiped away a tear and took a deep breath. "There's one thing I'd love to do. Let's get out on the water and away from all these people and craziness."

"Now that's a damn good idea. Best I've heard in a long time. Let's get back to the yacht, and we'll go into seclusion for a few days." His eyebrows raised and he kissed her hand.

"No...I'm taking you on my boat this time," she countered.

"Your boat? I didn't know you had one."

"It's Auntie's—it's my mother's boat. That's the first time I've said it. Wow, does that sound strange. It's moored off Manomet Beach. It's a little jaunt down the bluff, but easy to get to. Captain Maz said Auntie's friends were using it until I got back. Game?"

"Show me the way."

The atmosphere instantly lifted. She tried to erase the horrific memories of last night. Fresh ocean air would hopefully heal and revitalize her badly damaged soul.

On the other side of the coin, finding out the truth about her biological parents answered many questions. Their bond had always been special, especially time spent on the water. With Auntie and Captain Maz her parents, she was destined to be a seagoer. It saddened her she'd never get a chance to let Auntie know it was all okay, but the dear woman probably already knew that.

"Here, pull in this empty lot. See those stairs there? That's where we'll go down."

"Well, isn't this a spiffy set up. Parking lot, firewood, and boat storage. Wonder if he wants to sell this lot?"

"Fat chance. A family's owned this land for generations. They'll never part with it. They're nice enough to let a select few use their stairs to access the boats and beach."

"They're generous to let everyone use it."

They jumped out of the truck, and she grabbed the small cooler she'd purchased at the store. The elevation was higher than most spots on the Cape. On clear days, she could see the monument in P'town; the entire arm of the cape flexed northeast.

A gloomy morning, both weather-wise and emotionally, had turned into a fabulous afternoon with clear skies and satiny breeze.

Rod was winded by the time they hit the sand. One-hundred-two steps, including two landings, last time she counted.

They slipped off their shoes, and he rolled up his expensive pants. She sank her toes in the warm golden rocky sand. A white dinghy, upside down next to the stairs, leaned on the rocks. She grabbed the axle with double wheels and pulled it away. She flipped it over.

"Here, let me help you with that."

"Sure, if you want to drag it down to the water, that'd be great."

Seashells and rocks grinded against the hull. He made his way to the shoreline where gently lapping waves caressed the sand and rocks.

"I'm impressed. I had no idea you were a water babe," he teased. She threw her shoes in the boat.

"Water babe? Exactly what does that mean?"

"Someone that knows watercraft and how to operate them. If you show off your hot bod, that makes you a super water babe."

"Oh, I know how to operate more than you can imagine, Mr. Kesson," she flirted and wrapped her arm around his neck, placing a firm kiss on his lips.

"Is that right, Ms. Goddard." He reached around and pulled her close to his chest and tilted his head so the kiss was meaningful and deep.

"If you don't stop that, we may not get very far in the water," she warned.

"Fine by me."

"Seriously now. I'll get in the middle and let me get situated with the oars. Then you can push us out enough you can climb in without getting wet or hurt. I'll row us out. Can you do that without tipping us over?"

"Who do you think you're talking to? I'm the original Eagle Scout." Fumbling to get in, he splashed cold water on her and almost flipped the boat over when he jumped in.

She rowed out to sea, not breaking a sweat.

"So, which boat is your aunt's—I mean your mother's? The Rinker cruiser over there?"

"Nope. The one I'm rowing straight for."

"You mean that sailboat? What does it say? *Tinker Belle?*"

"It's a gaff rigged catboat and best in the fleet. This is the boat I learned to sail on and will always have a special place in my heart."

"I'm not being judgmental here, but looks a tad small to my liking. You sure you know what you're doing?"

"Trust me. I know more about sailing than you'll ever learn. Had the best teacher ever. Auntie." She glanced over at him. "Mom. Seems strange not to have Elly May with us though. She never missed a day lobstering. She'd hop in the skiff and onto the big boat, first mate. She was a big help culling crabs and trimming bait, that sweet girl. I'm glad she spends all of her time with Captain Maz—I mean Dad. It's going to take a while to get used to calling them that."

The water was incredibly calm, satin like, clear deep down. Seaweed swayed when disturbed by the paddles. Most years near a hundred boats were moored off Manomet Beach, used by local residents and guests.

It didn't take long to reach *Tinker Belle*. "I need you to carefully and slowly sit on this side of the dinghy right here while I hold the boat." A familiar tingle of excitement overpowered her.

"You won't push away just as I'm trying to get on to see if I can swim, will you?" he teased.

"And, can you swim?"

"Honestly, not that well, so let's not try it."

"I'd never do that to you." She clowned around and rocked the dinghy back and forth.

He wasted no time and quickly climbed aboard.

"Here, take this painter. Don't let go of it. Hold on to the side so I can get on," she instructed.

"Payback is hell, you know."

"Don't even consider it," she warned. "You don't want to mess with the captain."

Over the years it'd become more difficult to physically do what she had as a teenager, but she was ambitious enough not to let anything stop her.

After she struggled to get all her body parts in, she cleared the coaming and landed roughly on the inside wooden seat. She grabbed the painter and clipped it to the mooring up front, careful not to slip, unhooked the shackle which held *Tinker*, and threw off the safety clove hitch.

"Anything I can do to help?"

"Nope...just sit still 'til I get everything situated and then we'll be on our way."

She could impress him and pull out the sails, but instead pressed the button on the Honda ten-horse four-stroke long shaft. She was grateful the neighbors had used the boat and kept the battery charged, which made the engine easy to start.

It sputtered a few times while it warmed up then lollygagged quietly away from the dinghy and headed to open sea.

"I thought you had to pull a chord for those things to start?"

"And you know about boats? Here...steer for a minute. Can you handle a hardwood tiller?" she asked.

"Sure." His eyebrows shifted up and down.

She unlatched and entered through the maroon double doors to the cabin below, returning with two bottles of Sam Adams from the cooler.

"Like a beer?"

"How'd you know that was my favorite?"

"Just a guess." She popped off the lids using the opener mounted on the side of the cabin. She scooted close to him and stared off into the horizon. It was all water with a small lighthouse at the end of Gurnet Point.

"Doesn't get any better than this. I love the peace and serenity of the ocean. There's just something about it. I think I might have been a mermaid in a former life."

"Mermaid, huh? I think I was a whale. I had a big presence, you know." Rod pulled her onto his lap and wrapped his strong arms tightly around her.

She'd not been this content for a long time. Rod was a man she trusted. In the short time they'd been together, he'd proved his feelings were genuine. Was it possible to find two soul mates in one lifetime?

She gazed into his alluring eyes and kissed him ardently, hoping he'd understand how important he was to her. When he reciprocated, there was no doubt, none at all. He knew.

It was an awe-inspiring sunset. To the west the large orange oval slid behind the outline of the trees on the bluff, shedding brilliant hues of orange, yellow, and copper which reminded her of fall colors in the Midwest.

When she glanced to the east toward the tip of P'town, a full moon was rising. Colors were opposite in pastels of teal, blue, and mauve.

"Did you see that?" He pinched her leg.

"What?"

"I swear, there's a creature over there. Look, there's another one."

"I think you're imagining things. I don't see anything."

"Look...right over there. And now there's three," he insisted excitedly.

"Oh, those are seals. If we sit really still, they may follow us. Sometimes there are large pods. And if they get close, they make sounds like prehistoric animals snorting."

She turned off the engine, not wanting to scare or injure the sleek creatures. They sat quietly while the boat drifted. She'd often wondered how they'd respond if she slipped into the water with them. Would they frolic freely and sense she was an animal lover?

Their smooth and silky skin reflected the light which reminded her of leopard spots. Long whiskers emphasized elongated faces. Their large brown eyes were keen and watched every movement. They slowly disappeared one at a time into the depths to reappear closer to the dawdling boat.

"So missed all of this. This is what I've been looking for since I got here. Serenity. I should've taken the boat out before now. What was I thinking?" she sighed.

"You've been a little busy with a few responsibilities on your plate. Yes, this is heavenly, even though I'm used to a little more space and substance."

"So, Mr. Kesson, if you had to make a choice would it be the yacht or the lady with the little old boat?"

He chugged his beer and placed the glass bottle on the cockpit sole. He pulled her close, took her chin into his hand, and gazed into her eyes while he wrapped his arms around her and squeezed.

He kissed her without reservations. It was like a movie with the perfect romantic setting and the perfect man, the man she'd fallen in love with.

"I pick the lady. I love you, Kelli Goddard. I love everything about you. I've finally found my soul mate after all these years. You put me through hell, but you're worth it."

"Oh, is that so? Well, don't let this go to your head, but I love you too, Rod. But, I have to admit. I'm scared of loving again and getting hurt."

The kiss lingered and was intoxicatingly hot. The sun slowly set over the horizon while the rising moon witnessed their love.

"Always remember, if you fall, I will catch you," Rod whispered in her ear while a falling star dashed in front of the full moon.

EPILOGUE

Eighteen months later

Today was monumental in Kelli's book, other than the birth of her son and grandbabies, and the day she found out Hattie was her mother and Captain Maz her father. It didn't get any better than this.

It saddened her Auntie hadn't lived to share the truth, which would have enabled Auntie to share more in her family's lives. But, the dear woman was a guardian angel and watched over them.

She truly couldn't believe this was finally happening. People milled around the yard under the big white tents a local awning company had donated for this special occasion. Caterers set up tables, chairs, and food. Cars parked across the street where Stowell's Café and Deli's owner had granted permission and crowds mingled on the lush lawn. Katsura Gardens, who had done the incredible landscaping around the refurnished mansion and grounds, had come earlier in the morning to set up brilliant multi-colored pots of mums, which lined the sidewalk to the front entrance.

She perused herself in the mirror. The last six plus years had been brutal on her face and body. The drama and danger had taken an emotional toll, plus the physical demands of restoring the mansion. Was it worth it?

Hell, yes.

She smiled while applying the final touches of mascara and pink lipstick with clear gloss. She tussled her scrunched hair, trying to achieve a natural bounce.

Around her neck was a locket given to her by Rod. He surprised her one evening as they made plans for the big celebration. It contained a picture of Auntie and Captain Maz. She noticed immediately the resemblance to the one she'd seen Belinda wear. It would be a piece of history for her granddaughters to share.

The jewelry's simplicity accentuated the strapless red satin gown, a huge bow in the front tied off with a brooch of diamonds, an extravagant gift from Rod at Christmas. She slipped on above-the-elbow white gloves and red satin flats that would be hidden under the full skirt of the dress.

It was a dazzling warm fall day, the sun accented brown, gold, and red leaves. A perfect day in every regard. The windows were open which allowed fresh air to penetrate every corner in the newly restored mansion.

Her bedroom, painted pastel sea foam green, was a far cry from the shredded wallpaper and cracked plaster walls when she moved to town.

The hand-crafted four poster bed matched the massive headboard. All accessories in the room were white, which gave a clean and garden-fresh appearance. The comforter was made from squares of wrinkled cotton sewn together with a puff in the middle. Each piece had been handpicked by Rod and her.

This was the moment she'd waited for. She sprayed on Light Blue and excitedly pranced down the hall and stairs. The view was wondrous from every angle. The mansion had been restored inside and out to its original grandeur, accented with antiques handpicked to mimic her mother's furniture down to handmade afghans. Crochet circles dotted the furniture.

Everything sparkled, not only from being cleaned, but the sunshine added an extra gleam. When she opened the front door, she marveled at how many people strolled on the beautifully landscaped lawn.

Tents had been set up in front of the new barn, the last constructed piece on the estate. Its open doors exposed tables and chairs draped in white linens, accented by branches of pines, mums, sea horses, and shells. Laughter, chatter, and soft music infused the air.

She strolled on the wrap-around porch and paused to take in everything. She loved how the porch had been restored, leaving the curve uncovered and starburst floors. Everything was perfect. Not one detail had been overlooked.

Except Rod.

Where is he?

"Well, you did it, didn't you?" Gregg announced while he made his way up the porch.

"Guess we did, didn't we?" she replied with a wide grin.

"Kelli, I'll never be able to apologize enough for what my father did to you. I'll carry his burden all of my life and feel terrible he put you through all that. I hadn't seen or heard from him for a long time after he was released from prison and moved away. I hope you'll accept my sincere apologies. I hope you know I had nothing to do with it."

"Gregg, we've had this conversation before." She faced him and wrapped her arms around his slumped shoulders. "I know you didn't have anything to do with it. It's not your fault. You're not responsible for your dad's

255

actions. Don't let his misdoings follow you the rest of your life. Promise me? You're too good of a person to let it destroy you. I know you had a tough time growing up and now this, but you can move past it. You've had your battles, but you can overcome it. I know you."

"I'm really proud of you, Kelli. You took on a situation that most would've run from, but you didn't. I admire you. Always have and always will."

"Thanks, Gregg." His comments made her eyes mist.

"Well, this is quite an event, isn't it? You really outdid yourself."

"You bet it is. Have you seen Rod?"

"No, I haven't."

"Well, he's in deep shit. The festivities have started and he's nowhere to be found. Not like him to miss any part of this grand celebration of the mansion. He was more responsible for the restoration than me. He said he had to run an errand but would be right back. Guess we better join the festivities."

"I have to admit, I was wrong about Rod. He turned out to be a good guy. I'm glad it worked out between you two. Okey, dokey, let the party begin."

They strolled to the tents, arms interlocked. She smiled ear-to-ear while her heart pounded from excitement. She glanced over her shoulder to admire how beautiful the mansion had been restored.

Every dormer, window, French door, broken cornice, and shingle had been repaired or replaced by experienced craftsmen who specialized in restoring Victorian homes.

Rod had moved his motor coach to the back of the property where they lived while the house was being renovated. That gave them the opportunity to oversee every aspect of the project.

Amazingly, the situation settled down quickly after Adam Scott's death. Rod took the bull by the horn. With his expertise, connections, and financial support, he moved on the restorations quicker than she was prepared for. Occasionally, they'd escape the banging and barrage of carpenters and sail on *Tinker Belle* or his yacht, but she preferred *Tinker Belle* any day. Nothing else mattered as long as they were together.

They flew to South Carolina to meet his parents who fell madly in love with her and she them. Surprisingly, his father accepted Kelli with open arms. It took him a while to acknowledge and understand Rod's commitment to the restoration of the mansion, which meant the development of the condos was put on hold while they worked out details of their placement.

Captain Maz, with his failing health, decided he didn't want to maintain his acreage anymore. He sold to BKC for a development for low-income families that would only affect a small portion of the Cape, mostly covered in rocks.

He'd taken one of the units to keep an eye on the development, but Rod stepped up to the plate and offered to have all maintenance and repairs done for Captain Maz's lifetime. His life was complete with his daughter and Elly May. He'd even found outside religion and took the little dog to the Stations of the Cross at the local church's field. All the pieces had fallen together, thanks perhaps to the higher powers that guided them.

During the reconstruction and with the help of the map found in the upstairs chest, they'd discovered a fortune in silver ingots, coins, and artifacts hidden exactly where the map indicated. The items were donated to various causes and museums since Rod footed the entire bill for the inside and outside renovation of the estate.

As she approached the front tent, there were many unfamiliar faces. The group stopped chatting and stared. Her face grew warm.

One of the prerequisites of attending the unveiling of the mansion was to dress in 1800's era-appropriate attire. She loved the parasols, long skirts with hoops, ball gowns, gloves, and large hats or bonnets. Men were dressed in a variety of frockcoats, trousers, vests, dress brogans, and hats.

"Everyone, may I have your attention, please?" was announced over the loud speaker before she had a chance to speak to a single guest. Since everyone chatted loudly, it was announced a second time. The crowd simmered down.

She was so proud of Captain Maz. Shortly after he had stent surgery, he immediately had the paternity test completed. He was, in fact, her biological father. Both their lives and families had been enriched by the news.

Captain Maz tried to gain the crowd's undivided attention. "Thank you for coming today to help us celebrate this monumental occasion. Most of you know there's quite the story to the Manomet Mansion and anyone from town knows how much this property and home meant to Hattie and this community. Kelli and Rod have worked tirelessly to restore the house and grounds back to its original beauty and—"

The crowd clapped, whistled and raised their hands which interrupted his speech.

"This project was one most wouldn't have undertaken. We all knew how badly deteriorated this beautiful old lady was. Look at her now in all her grandeur and glory.

"So, today we graciously accept Kelli and Rod's overwhelmingly generous donation of this beautiful barn to be used by the residents of Manomet. And if that isn't enough, they've gifted the adjoining fifty acres to the village for parks, walking trails, and access to Manomet Beach plus a generous maintenance endowment."

The crowd roared. Men's hats flew into the air.

"So, Kelli and Rod, would you please come to the stage?"

She swiped at the tears with her fingertips, forgetting the white gloves. Captain Maz offered a hand while she climbed the three broad steps, hugged her, and placed a kiss on her damp cheek.

Where's Rod? I need you right now.

Captain Maz stepped away from the podium and left her on the stage by herself. She scoured the group for Rod. She didn't do well in crowds and wasn't prepared to make a speech, which Rod had agreed to do.

I'm about ready to have a panic attack. Rod. Where are you?

The crowd turned around when a vintage truck snaked up the newly asphalted driveway which led to the barn. The roadster appeared in mint condition, an REO Speedwagon, New England's first school bus.

She didn't recognize who was driving since he wore an old hat and jacket of the era. The lady in the front seat was barely visible. Someone she could barely see sat behind the driver. The truck pulled up. Everyone cheered and clapped. Was this supposed to be part of the celebration?

She didn't recognize Rod in his attire until he stood in front of the stage and faced her. The crowd silenced.

What's going on? Her legs trembled.

"Kelli Goddard. You are the most incredible woman I've ever met. When our paths crossed, I had no idea what an impact you'd have on my life. You've taught me so much that I was missing out on in life. I finally learned at this age it wasn't the material things that mattered, but family, peace, and goodwill. With this audience as my witness, I confess I'm not always right."

The crowd laughed and clapped.

"Restoring the mansion has been an incredible journey from many aspects, but with your guidance, insight, and endurance, and against all odds, it's been completed.

"Together, we rebuilt history. It's a legacy for your family and a tribute to Hattie and those before her. It will be passed on to your son, your granddaughters and generations to follow."

She almost fell off the stage when she recognized her beautiful granddaughters in long, fluffy pastel dresses, matching hats and parasols, her son and daughter-in-law in their apparel.

"We not only rebuilt a house, but we saved a home and in the process formed a loving partnership between two people that cannot be destroyed." He bent on one knee and took off his hat.

A distinguished elderly man and petite woman stood on each side of him. His father towered over Rod while his mother dabbed a handkerchief at her tears.

"I, Rod Kesson, would like for you to be my wife. I love you with all my heart. I want to spend the rest of my life with you. Will you marry me?" He pulled out a white velvet box, flipped open the lid which exposed a wide band covered in pink diamonds.

She was speechless, her vision blurred from the moisture she tried to contain by not blinking. Her legs shook under her long gown. "Yes, Rod Kesson. I will marry you—if my father will give me away."

Rod leaped onto the stage and kissed her like no man had ever kissed a woman, passionately and sincerely.

His parents hugged and cried openly while the crowd cheered. They embraced the bride and groom-to-be on stage with her son and family. She motioned Captain Maz to the platform and kissed him.

The festivities that day and evening would be in her memories forever. Not only did the celebration for the mansion turn out beyond her wildest expectations, but she gained a fiancée and wonderful in-laws in the process. His parents were ecstatic to finally have an extended family.

After the last person left, Rod helped his parents and her kids settle in the guest suites. She was exhausted. It'd been a long time since she'd truly been that happy and content.

The weather had cooperated with not only a calm sunny day, but now the sky was lit up by a full moon. Stars dotted the darker part of the sky where occasional puffs of cloud drifted over.

When she strolled up the sidewalk to the mansion from the barn, she instinctively looked up at the widow's walk, forever her favorite spot in the house.

She blinked a couple of times. Was it her imagination or were people on the widow's walk?

~ ~ ~

Belinda spotted Kelli while she stood on the widow's walk. She swaddled her daughter in her arms while Joshua embraced them both.

For over a century her spirit had roamed under the wicked moon, unable to complete the journey and pass to the next plane. With Kelli's help, lies had been exposed. Joshua had been released from his hidden grave, setting him free to finally reunite with his lost love.

They faced the full moon. Life had come full circle for all of them.

Would you like to see a sequel to *Wicked Moon*?
Let Taylor Nash know at
taylor@taylornash. com

Follow Taylor via her website, blog, and twitter.

If you haven't read **Uncharted Depths** and **The
Apparition**, they are available at
Booklocker.com, taylornash.com or wherever
books are sold
and also available in Ebook Format.

~ ~ ~

Arrangements for tours or events can be made
at directors@simeshousefoundation.org.

A virtual tour, membership in the Foundation,
history, pictures and apparel can be found by
visiting the website
www.simeshousefoundation.org/.

CPSIA information can be obtained at www.ICGtesting.com
Printed in the USA
LVOW04s0014110914

403400LV00003B/3/P